*Matty and the
Problem Ponies*

Matty and the Problem Ponies

by Jane Ayres

Published by Pony, Stabenfeldt A/S
Cover illustration: Jennifer Bell
Cover layout: Stabenfeldt AS
Typeset by Roberta L. Melzl
Editor: Bobbie Chase
Printed in Germany 2005

ISBN: 1-933343-18-4

Stabenfeldt, Inc.
457 North Main Street
Danbury, CT 06811
www.pony.us

Chapter 1

"Sweet, placid and 100% in every way." That was the description in the sale catalogue of our new pony, Comfort. Of course, if this had turned out to be the case, then I don't suppose I would have a tale to tell, because it would have been very simple, really, a happy ever after story. *Girls buy pony, pony is perfect, end of story.*

Hmmm.... Well, if I was the sort of person who gets easily downhearted in situations of adversity... But, of course, I am not like that.

"Matty, I wish you weren't so impulsive. It will get you into trouble one of these days." *(My mom.)*

"For goodness' sake, Matty Mathews, use some common sense. Try to be a bit less naive." *(My dad.)*

"I can't understand why you girls waste all your time

on ponies. There's no future in it, and no career prospects." *(My school Guidance Counselor.)*

"Don't call me Veronica – not even for a joke – if you want to keep all your teeth." *(My best friend, Ronnie, who, as you will have gathered, hates being named Veronica.)*

"Can I borrow your hairbrush again?" *(My friend, Gina, who is a bit vain.)*

"If I have to muck out one more stable, I swear I'll...!" *(You don't want to hear the rest. That's Spike, another of our pony-mad girl gang.)*

"I'm so lucky to be going out with a girl like you." *(My boyfriend, Mark. I admit, he hasn't actually said these exact words to me, although I'm sure he would if he thought about it...)*

And finally – "You really are the best rider I have ever encountered." *(OK, so that's what I tell myself. Modesty is not a problem I suffer from.)*

So here we are, several months after I set off intrepidly with Ronnie, Spike and Gina to the local horse sale, clutching our cash, madly excited and impatient to buy our new pony. On the face of it, Comfort certainly appeared to meet our criteria. She was eight years old, 14.2 hands high, light bay with a pretty head, a kind eye, cheap to run (a mountain breed, so she could live outdoors) and just within our price range. Bringing her home, we were over the moon.

So, how many prizes have we won on our new pony? Is she a good jumper? Handy at gymkhana games? An exciting ride?

The simple answer is – we don't know! Not yet, anyway.

I'll update you. My name is Matty Mathews. I am fourteen years old and pony mad. I have blue eyes and short mousey brown hair, unlike my best friend, Ronnie, who lives next door and who has pretty emerald eyes and a mane of copper-gold hair. She, too, is crazy about horses, as is Spike, who is very brainy, dresses like a boy, and has short-cropped hair and six stud earrings in each ear. Finally, Gina, who is the biggest contrast to Spike that you could imagine, being ultra feminine, with delicate features and pale eyes like a fragile doll, rounds out our quartet. Gina's mother sometimes fusses over her as if she were about six years old. She does not approve of Spike and dislikes horses, which makes life a bit difficult for Gina at times. Oh, and I nearly forgot Mark, my boyfriend. He has dark, curly hair and gorgeous eyes. We've been going out for a year now and we still get along! Perhaps it is true love...

How we came to buy Comfort is a long story, but I will give you a brief run-down. Last summer, the four of us were walking back from the movies (having missed the last bus home), and decided to take a shortcut through the graveyard, where we found a wonderful runaway horse. Yes, *found*. I know it sounds unlikely, but that is exactly what happened. Well, we decided to keep this horse, who we called Moonlight, in secret up at the Old Fort. In those days, it was a derelict, creepy place, which was supposed to be haunted, and where no one went, so we knew it was safe for our horse. We schooled him and cared for him and it was wonderful, although we knew, deep down, that one day we would have to give him back, even though no one had reported him missing or stolen, which was surprising because he was a Thoroughbred. Anyway, to cut a long story short, I discovered by chance that he was a brilliant jumper and I rode him in a local show, and came in second in the jumping class, (losing to Mark, who rode in those days and had a wonderful mare called Snowstorm, whom I adored). I nearly got arrested by the police who claimed the horse was stolen, and finally had to surrender him to his rightful owner, which was very sad.

Moonlight turned out to be Socrates, an ex-show jumper who appeared in TV commercials, and his owner, Carly, was so pleased to get him back that she gave us a generous cash reward. Which, of course, we used to buy our own pony.

It turned out that Mark's dad was a horsey person, and he bought the Old Fort and converted it into a riding school, which he runs. This was all fine and good with us, as Miss Pugh's old stables, where we all spent most of our waking hours, even though she was a strange eccentric woman who really didn't much like horses, were sold to Miss Pugh's fiancée Eric so that he could expand his used car lot next door.

So we got Comfort from a local horse sale and led her home in triumph, only to find that by the next day she was lame. This was an unexpected blow, but the vet assured us that we had not bought a basically unsound mare; it was more likely that she had stepped on a piece of gravel or something, and that had caused the minor injury. She advised complete rest. So we let Comfort settle in at her new home as a boarder at The Old Fort Stables, and wrote off the next week or so as far as riding her was concerned. But the nights were already getting darker and darker, and wetter and wetter, and before we knew it, Christmas had arrived.

Then, finally, Comfort was pronounced sound. The vet decreed, "Light trail riding only to start with. She is broken in, isn't she?" It seemed like an odd sort of question.

"Of course," we chorused, although there was this

curious thought at the back of my mind that nowhere on any of the sale details had it said that Comfort had ever been ridden...

During this lengthy rest period, Comfort was turned out by day to eat grass and stabled at night to eat hay, apparently enjoying her days munching away. She made friends with Elliott, one of the riding school ponies who was turned out with her, and I blame Elliott for the alarming incident when she went missing for two days. Elliott has learned how to open the gate with his teeth, so a special Elliott-proof lock was added to the gate. However, on this occasion, a new helper at the stables put him away at night and forgot about the additional security. Hence, the next day we arrived to find an empty field. Panic ensued and a frantic search began. Elliott was consequently recovered at the local garden center. Alone. We tracked down Comfort, eventually, in a field miles away. Although we had all been worried sick, as you can imagine, she returned home looking as nonchalant as ever, wondering what all the fuss was about. Where she went and what she did on those two days was a complete mystery. However, the consequences of her little escapade have a bearing on the story, as you will see later.

Although she did get some exercise during her "rest" period, (we all took turns taking her out on the lead rope for a stroll each day), not surprisingly, she got fat and Mark started to refer to her as our Pudding Pony, which I did not find amusing.

"I so want to see what she's like to ride," complained Gina.

"Yes, I know, we all do. It's disappointing for everyone. We just have to be patient, that's all," said Ronnie.

And at last the day came, and we were able to take turns riding Comfort.

I have to say, she was not the ride we had expected.

To prevent squabbling, we tossed a coin to decide who would ride her first, and Spike won the toss. Comfort seemed most put out to have a saddle on her back and she kept rolling her eyes and pulling faces at us.

"She probably thought her little vacation would last forever," remarked Gina, giggling. She was excited at the prospect of a ride on Our New Pony. Ronnie looked a little cautious. I think she was more observant than the rest of us, and she had noticed that Comfort was not as keen as we were.

Spike went to tighten the girth and Comfort glared and laid back her ears.

"I'll hold her head," offered Ronnie thoughtfully.

Honestly, if a pony could moan like a human, then I'm sure that's what Comfort would have done by now. She did look grumpy.

Spike carefully lowered herself into the saddle, thanked Ronnie, and gathered up the reins. We were in the outdoor ring, and although the sky was bluish, dark clouds hovered, threatening rain.

Comfort gave a little snort when Spike pressed her legs against her sides.

But she didn't walk on.

"Could you all move back to the fence, if you don't mind," asked Spike. "We don't want to crowd her."

We all obligingly retired to the fence, Gina sitting on it, me leaning against it and Ronnie standing alert. I felt a little apprehensive for some reason.

Still, Spike was a strong and competent rider, so what could possibly go wrong?

We all watched as Spike pressed again with her legs, harder this time, but Comfort just stood and stared into space. Exasperated, Spike started to kick.

"Don't do that," shouted Ronnie disapprovingly. "You're flapping. You'll lose all contact with her."

"Frankly, I don't think I had any in the first place,"

retorted Spike. "Come on, girl," she urged our new pony.

"Stubborn little mare, isn't she?" grinned Mark, appearing as if from nowhere.

"What, Comfort?" I asked mischievously.

"Well, I didn't mean Spike," he laughed. "Stop it, you two," hissed Ronnie. "I think we have a problem here."

After five tedious minutes, Spike gave up and dismounted. "She just won't move."

"Give her a whack," suggested a teenage boy who had just arrived for a private lesson with Mark's dad.

We all looked shocked. None of us has ever used a crop on a pony. It was a vow we all made and stick to rigidly.

"What's the problem?" asked Mark.

"The problem is, this pony has sides of iron," replied Spike. "It's like sitting on an immovable object, like a lump of wood."

"Would anyone else care to try?"

I looked at Mark. He was the best rider I knew, if a bit mechanical. He read my thoughts.

"No, sorry, Matty. You know I've given up riding. Why don't you give it a try?"

"Yes, try, Matty," encouraged Gina.

So I took the reins from Spike and mounted Comfort.

I crossed the stirrups over the front of the saddle, as I often prefer to ride without them, feeling it gives me more contact with the horse. I squeezed her sides, but there was no response at all. I played with the reins to see how sensitive her mouth was, but there was no reaction.

"I don't think she knows what to do," observed Ronnie. "I don't think she's ever been schooled."

"She's eight. She must have been," I replied, although logically this was not necessarily the case.

Ronnie stepped forward and started to lead Comfort around the school, at which point she plodded on, head down. But when Ronnie let go, Comfort just stopped again.

"She's lazy," muttered Gina. "Or a slug," added Spike.

"I don't understand it," I said.

Then Ronnie said what none of us wanted to hear.

"I hate to say this, but there is something not quite right about Comfort. We might have gotten ourselves a dud pony."

"Not dud," interrupted Mark. "Just green. She's inexperienced, unschooled."

It did, indeed, appear as if Comfort had hardly been ridden, let alone schooled. Visions of winning prizes at the next local show began to fade into oblivion.

"Cheer up," said Mark. "You all have a great opportunity to develop Comfort into the pony you want. It may be a long, slow process, but it will be worth it in the end. Any horse can be improved by patient, careful schooling. But don't expect instant success."

His words of wisdom were delivered with a certain smugness, I thought, but even so, we all knew that Mark was right.

And so began Comfort's training. She didn't object too much to having someone on her back, and she never actually bucked (although she was thinking about it sometimes, you could tell the way she tensed her back), and she had clearly been handled a fair amount. Mark thought that she had probably been bought as a youngster by someone who handled and backed her, but then didn't have much time for her, so just turned her out in the paddock and left her alone. She didn't mind people, but she wasn't used to being worked. And this was going to present us with something of a problem.

So far, we had been shelling out our combined pocket money to keep Comfort at the stables as a full boarder, until she had recovered from her lameness. The idea then was that she would be a working boarder, giving riding lessons in the daytime while we were at school, to contribute to her keep. Of course, this was now out of the question.

Although Mark wouldn't ride, he did give us advice about schooling Comfort, and helped us with a program that we all hoped would transform our mare. It involved lunging every day, with short periods of riding in the ring. We all took turns lunging and riding her, and I think of the four of us, Ronnie and I had the most success. I don't mean to sound bigheaded about this, but Spike was too impatient and Gina wasn't firm enough, letting Comfort get away with murder. It took seemingly forever to teach Comfort to lead with the inside leg when cantering in a circle, and Ronnie's first successful turn on the forehand was a cause of considerable celebration. Any progress was gradual but slow. Painfully slow.

So here we are, just a few weeks away from Spring break. Mom and Dad have been looking forward to taking a little break themselves. Dad is always moaning about his job in town, and Mom is still doing her job share at the local council offices with her friend, Angie. I hope I never have to do a job I don't particularly enjoy. Dad pointed out that if I ever get married, or buy a house, or have children, I'll have to be able to earn money, and that most people do a job they don't like in order to pay the bills. I vowed never to marry, or buy a house or have children. I would rather live in a tent in the woods with my horse and become a hermit.

I am sitting in the kitchen, visualizing a rustic little setup with a campfire and living off berries and fruit when Mom reminds me that soon Silke, my German pen pal, is due to arrive.

I have to admit (although not to Mom, who would be understandably shocked) that I had completely forgotten about this. I know it sounds awful, but there you go. My mind has been completely absorbed with Comfort, with no space for anything else.

"We can put the cot in your room so that you two girls can share," says Mom, who is looking forward to playing host. I must admit I can do without the hassle. Silke and I have been writing for nearly a year. We met through a pony mag pen pal page. At first, Silke wrote a lot about riding and the friend's pony that she looked after. It was fun, getting her letters, which tend to be much livelier and full of events than mine. But lately, she hasn't mentioned horses nearly as much. She seems to be more concerned about pop stars and clothes. Still, it will be fun showing her Comfort and the Old Fort and introducing her to Gina, Spike and Ronnie.

"She's staying for three weeks, isn't she?" asked Mom.

I nod. In return, during the summer, I can go and stay with Silke. I wonder what it will be like; sharing my room with someone I have never actually met.

I guzzle juice and rush off the to The Old Fort to meet the others. It is my turn to muck out Comfort and clean her tack.

The new indoor ring looks fantastic, with floodlights and gallery seating, lots of space and a new set of show jumps. There is talk of a cross-country course being ready for the summer. Mark's dad (who we all used to think of as a bit of tyrant) has done wonders with The Old Fort Stables. It is his baby, Mark says, his new business venture and a labor of love, and he has put all of his money into it. I wish I could persuade Mark to ride again, but he focuses his energies on practising his clarinet. Mark never liked riding, and only used to ride to please his dad. And the irony is that it was me who encouraged him to stand up to his dad and tell him that he would rather be a musician than a show jumper. Still, that's life, I suppose. Things never turn out the way you expect. Mark plays in the same amateur jazz band as my dad, who also plays clarinet, and Ronnie's dad, who is a drummer. At this point I should add that both of my parents think the world of Mark. However, secretly, they probably wonder what he sees in me. I wonder myself sometimes.

Still, at least Mark helps out at the stables, so we get to spend plenty of time together. Watching Mark sitting on the gate, his legs dangling casually while he munches an apple, I recall the first time I set eyes on him. It was when I had sneaked a ride on his gorgeous gray pony, Snowstorm, and been caught in the act. He really laid into me then, but despite my embarrassment and instant dislike of his arrogant manner, I still couldn't help noticing his lovely black curly hair and sad brown eyes. His dad had come across as really overbearing, and a bit of a bully, and called me a silly kid, which, as you can imagine, made me furious. It seems like ages ago now, but it was only last summer. And I never forgot Snowstorm, who Mark finally sold when he decided to give up riding. I recall the day I was left alone at the rundown riding stables where we used to spend all our waking hours, when Snowstorm had nuzzled my hair and licked my hands affectionately. She was a dream of a pony. I still wonder what became of her. Mark said she went to a good, knowledgeable home, but I wish he hadn't sold her. To make up for it in some small way, Mark gave me a lovely framed photograph of Snowstorm for a Christmas present. It captures her perfectly; her neat ears, dish face and liquid brown eyes like pools that melt you as you gaze into them. I keep it by my bedside, and have to admit that I kiss this picture every night before I go to sleep. It is the only bit of Snowstorm I have left. Secretly, I hope that one day I will find her again.

While I am mucking out the stable, Mark kindly takes Comfort into the yard and gives her a brush and picks out her feet.

"Do you want to go out tonight?" he asks. "There's a new movie out, a big adventure story with tons of special effects. We could go into town this afternoon."

I nod. "That sounds like fun." It is Saturday. Mark and I usually go out somewhere together on Saturday. It has become one of our routines.

While we are chatting, Ronnie and Gina appear, leading Polo, Mia and Cy.

"Have either of you seen Spike? Mark's dad has asked us to take a trail ride out for him, but we can't find Spike. She would normally jump at the chance to ride Polo." Polo is currently Spike's favorite pony, after Comfort. She has talked of the possibility of having him on loan some time in the distant future.

"I haven't seen her today," I reply. "Funny, she's usually here by now."

"Spike is usually the first one here," agrees Ronnie. "Not like us lazy bunch, who prefer our beds on a Saturday morning."

They hang around for a while, and then have to leave to take the trail ride.

"We'll put Polo in his stall and leave him tacked up, so if she arrives soon she can catch up to us," offers Gina.

Not long after, Spike turns up. She doesn't look very happy and her eyes are red and puffy.

"Hey, Spike," I greet her. "You just missed the trail ride, but Polo is ready and waiting for you." She doesn't respond.

"Is anything wrong?" I ask gently. It is hard to imagine, but it looks as if Spike has been crying. Even so, neither Mark nor I dare to suggest this.

"Yes, there is," she replies, taking out a hanky and blowing her nose.

"Dad has been offered another job. A really good one."

"You've lost me, Spike," I begin tactlessly. "How is that so awful?"

Spike glares at me and snaps, "Because his new job is in Paris. He has to start as soon as possible, so we all have to move to France. Next month, to be precise."

Chapter 2

I have never seen Spike so upset. Actually I don't think I have *ever* seen Spike upset at all. She is normally one of those resilient sort of people who seem to be permanently cheerful and positive.

It is hard to take in what she is saying. "But you can't move away from here," I begin. "I mean, we have our pony now, and..."

"You have to tell your parents you can't go away," adds Gina, who is devastated. Spike is her closest friend.

"Don't you think I've tried that?" Spike replies. "We've been arguing ever since Dad gave us the news. I know I should be happy for him, because it's a great job, but –"

"You're perfectly entitled to be upset," consoles Ronnie.

We all stand awkwardly for a while. I am shuffling from one foot to the other in uncomfortable silence. Spike senses this and lets us off the hook by saying, "Well, I think I'll take Polo out and try to catch up with the others for the trail ride. Usual route, I expect."

"Poor Spike," I murmur when she is out of earshot.

After Spike's news there is a cloud of doom hanging over us. At lunchtime, when Ronnie and I are sitting in the tack room, eating our sandwiches, we try not to think about what it will be like without Spike, and I recall how we used to spend all our time at the ratty old stables I mentioned earlier. Anyway, when Miss Pugh pulled her dirty trick on us, as we saw it, Mark's father stepped in to rescue the riding school ponies, which now reside happily at the Old Fort Stables. I have a soft spot for all of them, but particularly the cheeky skewbald escape artist Elliot, and Soames, the jealous cobby bay with enormous feet. Then there's moody old Bessie who has gotten fatter and meaner than ever, and is entirely ungrateful for her new home; Everest, the ex-show pony, reputedly a champion in his younger day (he's now a pensioner, and only used for light trail riding); and Cy, the frisky bay who likes to be chased. I still miss Penny, the chestnut, who was bought by one of the students, but Mark's dad acquired some new additions to the stables, and with his expert horseman's eye made some great choices (now why didn't we take him to the horse sale when we bought Comfort? I suppose we thought we knew it all...) The pair of Shetlands called Bumper and Binky that Mark's dad got for the very young riders are really cuddly. Then he bought two Thoroughbreds, Mia and Sovereign, and another cob, a real sweetie called Lydia, for the adult riders, all chestnuts (he likes chestnuts).

Spike is very keen on Polo, a flea-bitten gray Connemara mare with a super jump.

"I think Spike sometimes wishes we had Polo instead of Comfort, particularly when Comfort shied at the far corner of the ring for the seventeenth time," observes Ronnie. "I can't imagine her moving away from here. We will all miss her so much."

"Maybe her parents will change their minds," I wonder, but from what Spike said earlier that sounds very unlikely.

When Ronnie and I have finished eating, we have an unsuccessful schooling session with Comfort, as Everest, who is grazing in the nearby paddock, continually distracts her. He is ignoring her, but she can't take her eyes off him for some reason, so her concentration on learning to halt and walk on when asked is practically nil.

Finally, since Comfort is in a particularly uncooperative mood, we both decide it is pointless to continue and call it a day. After untacking her, we turn her out in the end paddock on her own. I'm not sure which one of us was responsible for shutting the gate. As you will see later on, this will come back to haunt us.

"I won't be able to get to the stables tomorrow," says Ronnie, whose plans for the evening revolve around a hot bath followed by crashing on the couch to watch a horror flick on TV. "Mom and Dad have to go and visit a sick relative, so I'm stuck looking after the terrible twins."

"Poor you," I commiserate, glad that I don't have any younger siblings.

As Mark is coming around shortly to take me for a pizza before we go to the movies, I quickly shower and get changed into clean jeans and a floppy red sweater. I look at myself in the mirror and experiment a bit with a couple of necklaces and a scarf, but soon give it up. Some people are born with style. *I'm not one of them.*

When I go downstairs Mark has already arrived and is chatting away to Mom about school, the clarinet, life, the universe and everything. I don't know what he finds to talk about with Mom half the time. I can easily run out of conversation, but Mark has good social skills, as my Guidance Counselor would say.

Mom hastily scans me up and down and I can tell she is wishing I would dress up a bit and try to look more feminine – *"Make an effort,"* is what she would have liked to say, I think. Still, Mark doesn't seem too worried about such things.

"I've just been telling Mark about your pen pal coming to stay," says Mom cheerfully.

"Yes, you never said anything about her, Matty."

"I completely forgot," I reply, and it is perfectly true.

"What's she like?" he asks.

I frown. "How do I know? I've never met her. But she sounds nice from her letters. And she likes horses," I add, as if this is the most important thing.

"Enjoy yourselves, you two," calls Mom as I head for the door.

"We'll try," I reply, and I grab my purse and some clean tissues on my way out.

The movie isn't as exciting as I expect, although Mark seems to think so. I can't help fidgeting. The seat feels all itchy, the popcorn (we buy a king-sized bucket) tastes soggy, and I keep yawning. My mind is being overwhelmed with problems vying for attention – like Spike having to move away and Comfort's apparent learning difficulties. Luckily Mark is wrapped up in the movie and he doesn't seem to notice, although it must be irritating for the people sitting behind us every time I change position in the seat. Something has occurred to me about Spike, and I wish it hadn't. Of the four of us, Spike makes the biggest financial contribution toward Comfort's upkeep because she gets the most pocket money. So if she moves to France, we will have to share the costs between the three of us, and I'm not sure we can manage that. I wonder if this thought has occurred to any of the others. I feel very mean that it has occurred to me. In fact, I feel quite ashamed.

The next morning when I arrive at the stables, it being my turn to exercise Comfort, I find to my surprise that the field is empty.

"Comfort," I shout, although since there is only one tree I would see her if she was there. I peer into the lean-to shelter, expecting her to be munching hay, but she is nowhere to be seen. Feeling uneasy, I walk back to the yard and check her stall, but there is no sign of her. Puzzled, I spot Lisa, who is untacking her dun gelding, Crackerjack, and ask, "Do you know if Comfort has been moved?"

She shakes her head. "Sorry, I wouldn't know."

My feeling of unease is rapidly developing into definite concern. I go back to the field, hoping somehow that I will find Comfort unaccountably standing there, waiting for me. I put my hand out to push open the gate, which I discover is already slightly ajar. By now I am panicking, recalling the last occasion something like this happened. Only this time, Elliott is not to blame because he was stabled last night.

I try to recall yesterday, when we put Comfort back in the field after our less than fruitful schooling session. Did I shut the gate properly? I thought I had. Admittedly I had been preoccupied with the Spike situation. So had Ronnie. Come to think of it, was Ronnie the last out? If so, she was responsible for shutting the gate. Whatever had happened it was too late for recriminations. I had to raise the alarm.

As I ran back to the stables, I bumped into Spike and Gina who had just arrived.

"Comfort has gotten out!" I blurt breathlessly. "We have to find her!"

"Gotten out? How could she? Surely you closed the gate properly yesterday –"

"I thought I did," I snap back at Gina. "It might have been Ronnie. Anyway, the gate's been open and now it's swung shut again but the catch isn't secured, so clearly our pony is out there somewhere and we have to search for her before she gets hit by a car..."

"At least she's been microchipped, so if she turns up somewhere she can be traced back to us," interrupts Spike, trying to sound calm. That was how we had located her last time she went missing.

"We have to search the lanes first," I begin, my mind racing, visions of Comfort coming face to face with a truck on the busy main road crowding unwelcome into my mind.

"I'd better tell Mark's dad what's happened, just in case we're overreacting and he moved Comfort somewhere else without us knowing," suggests Gina suddenly.

"Like where? It doesn't seem likely," I respond angrily. I am annoyed at myself, unable to live with the fact that I may have been responsible for our pony getting out.

"Comfort may have been taken ill, be at the vet's," she replies and this worries me even more, but she has disappeared into the office to make sure we are not on a wild goose chase.

"We're wasting time," I say impatiently. "What if Comfort got out last night? She could be lying on a road somewhere while we are –"

Before I can finish my sentence Gina reappears with Mark's dad close behind.

"I've just had a phone call," he says gravely. I hardly dare breathe. "From Mrs. Green, on the edge of the new housing development."

29

Fearing the worst, I didn't want to hear the rest. Perhaps to block out what I thought was coming next, I pictured Mrs. Green, recalling that she lives in a big house and her daughter, Marcie, used to ride here before she got a job in Australia with a film production company.

Mark's dad continues. "She wanted to know if one of my horses got out, because a pony turned up in her yard this morning."

"Oh, thank goodness." I breathe a sigh of relief so loudly I'm surprised the whole yard doesn't hear it.

"We'll go and get her right away," insists Gina.

Mark's dad shakes his head. "I'm afraid it's not that simple."

"Oh. What do you mean?" asks Spike, and I wonder why life is never simple.

"What's the problem?" wonders Gina. "Why can't we go get our pony?"

"Because Comfort is currently..." he hesitates, wondering how to say it. "I can hardly believe this myself. Your pony has gotten into Mrs. Green's swimming pool."

Chapter 3

This came as a bit of a shock, to say the least.

"In the swimming pool? Are you sure that's what she said?"

"Yes, that is exactly what she said," replies Mark's dad somewhat impatiently.

"But how...?"

"Never mind that. We have to get over there quickly. She has already called the fire department."

"The fire department?"

"Matty, will you stop repeating everything I say! It's rather tiresome. Now, grab some rope and let's get over to Mrs. Green's house – now!"

My mind is still reeling as we pile into the four-wheel drive and race over to Mrs. Green's place. The idea of a pony in a swimming pool seems so bizarre that I don't immediately grasp the seriousness of the situation. I suppose also that I am relieved that Comfort is alive and well and not lying crushed beneath the wheels of a juggernaut.

We arrive to find Mrs. Green standing anxiously at the side of her very large outdoor swimming pool, talking reassuringly to Comfort who, to our horror, is trapped in the water, her head and neck visible above the surface.

"Oh, Comfort," I exclaim, rushing to her.

"She's shivering," observes Gina.

"That's not surprising. It's a cold morning, so the water must be freezing," points out Spike.

"Thank goodness you're here," says Mrs. Green urgently. She is a tall, trim woman, about my mom's age, and I notice that she is still wearing pajamas beneath her baggy sweater and coat. "I was asleep in bed when I heard a terrible commotion outside and the squeal of car brakes. I ran to the window just in time to see this pony gallop into the yard. I expect she got scared by the traffic and panicked. She didn't even see the swimming pool and plunged straight in. The water would have been hidden by the cover, so I suppose that confused her, and I thought the swimming pool cover might hold her weight, but it didn't."

I have a sudden thought. What if Comfort had actually

been hit by a car before she plunged into the pool? There would be no way of knowing until we got her out.

"I tried to coax her out at first, since she was in the shallow end," continues Mrs. Green. "But it was no use. I tried to grab her head collar to pull her, but it didn't work. She just kept throwing her head around. I did try," she repeats apologetically. "I realized I needed help so I decided to call the fire department. They should be here very soon."

"She might be caught in the netting," suggests Gina.

"What netting?" I respond.

"The netting beneath the pool cover," replies Mrs. Green.

I study the meshing floating on the water and see that Gina could be right.

"We can't just stand here," I protest. "We have to do something."

"We should wait for the fire department. They'll have the right equipment," advises Mark's dad.

"But they could be ages. They might get stuck in traffic," says Spike.

"Maybe while we're waiting for the fire crew to arrive, we could wade into the water to see if we can confirm whether the netting is caught around Comfort's legs."

Before anyone can stop us, Spike and I shed our boots and jackets and jump into the pool. Of course, in our haste we do entirely the wrong thing and the splashing we create panics Comfort even further and she starts to thrash in an agitated manner, which probably further tangles her in the mesh.

Also, the water is very cold and is a bit of a shock to the system.

With teeth chattering, we fumble underneath the surface of the water, unable to see what we are doing properly, in an attempt to locate the netting. Meanwhile Gina holds Comfort's head and tries to soothe her.

At this point, we hear loud sirens and, to our relief, the firemen arrive.

We are hauled out of the water and sit cold and wet by the pool, trying to keep our pony calm while they make repeated attempts to free her from the netting.

"It's wrapped around both hind legs," shouts one of the firemen. "Too tight to remove without cutting it, and we can't risk that in these conditions."

So the decision is made, with Mrs. Green's ready agreement, to drain all the water from the pool.

"I wouldn't have thought of that," murmurs Spike, shivering violently. Since we both refuse to go into the house to keep warm, not wanting to leave the scene for an instant in case Comfort is hurt, Mrs. Green fetches fluffy towels for us to wrap ourselves in.

"Once the pool is drained it will be over soon," ventures Gina.

As soon as the water level drops, the firemen get to work skilfully cutting the netting, which is tightly entwined around Comfort's legs. How they do it without hurting her, I'll never know. At least five of them hold her still while we all talk to her, just in case she moves at the wrong moment. But by now I think she is so numb by the experience that she seems dazed and stands like a statue.

"Good girl, clever girl," we all cry, and even the fireman are patting her and praising her. Bewildered, she blinks at us. Of course, we hadn't reckoned on how exactly a pony was going to scramble up a six foot wall to get out of the pool, even if drained.

"We're used to rescuing animals from lakes and rivers, but a horse in a swimming pool is a new situation," remarks the head fireman, frowning.

However, being resourceful, they build a ramp out of crates and planks of wood, which Mrs. Green locates in her huge garage. (We discover later that her husband, who is at work, is a builder). They eventually succeed in coaxing her, finally, out of the pool and back on terra firma. We are elated. The whole rescue operation has taken nearly two hours.

"Oh, thank you, thank you," we all cry, wanting to hug the firemen.

"All in a day's work – well, not usually," they joke.

Mrs. Green fetches hot drinks for everyone, and

while they pack up their equipment we check Comfort's legs, which seem remarkably unscathed, apart from surface cuts.

"Her hock looks swollen," I observe, realizing that I can't actually feel my lips, I am so cold.

"Oh, no, there's blood coming from Comfort's mouth," exclaims Gina in alarm.

I see the thin red trickle and my heart misses a beat. Luckily, Mark's dad steps in before we panic again.

"Hold her head," he instructs Spike, and he opens Comfort's mouth and peers inside.

"Nothing to worry about," he says calmly. "She's just bitten her tongue, probably when she got scared. But the vet will be here shortly, to check her over properly. Mrs. Green has already called him."

Luckily, his assessment turns out to be correct. The vet confirms that Comfort has escaped with a cut tongue, minor surface abrasions and a bruised hock and advises complete rest for at least a week.

While Mark's dad and Gina load Comfort into the horse trailer, Mrs. Green insists that Spike and I come inside to warm up.

"Here, put on some of these clothes that Marcie left behind," she offers. "You'll catch your death of cold, if you haven't already."

She ushers us into a big warm bathroom and we dry off gratefully. When we emerge I can see by her expression that she is thinking of her daughter Marcie, who she plainly misses.

"Still, they have to grow up and you have to let them go," she sighs wistfully. "When I was her age, you couldn't stop me from riding. I used to have my own horse when I was younger, a champion Thoroughbred. I do hope that your pony will recover from her terrible ordeal today."

"Thanks, but the vet assures us that Comfort will make a full recovery," I reply.

"I do feel bad about what happened, even though I know it was an accident," she begins. "But before you go, perhaps you would like to take something with you." She disappears briefly into Marcie's room and re-emerges with a pile of pony magazines.

"Marcie left these behind – I was going to give them to a charity shop, but I know you girls would appreciate them."

"That's really kind," I say. "Thank you."

By the time we travel back to the Old Fort and settle Comfort in a warm stable, we are all so tired that Mark's Dad sends us straight home, promising to keep an eye on our pony for us. Considering her ordeal, she seems quite calm, but I suppose she feels safe back in familiar surroundings and smells.

I call on Ronnie, who is still baby-sitting the twins and looking rather harassed, and tell her everything that has happened. Understandably she is worried.

"Are you sure that Comfort will be OK? I feel dreadful – I was sure I closed the gate properly, but maybe –"

"Look, it doesn't matter now which one of us was the last to close the gate. It could have been me. I honestly can't remember. We were both preoccupied with Spike. There's no point in feeling guilty, although it's natural that we will. You can be sure that both of us will be doubly careful to check the gate in the future."

Ronnie nods in agreement. "Absolutely."

Back home, I soon end up asleep on the sofa in front of the TV after a long hot bath. "Why don't you go to bed, dear?" Mom suggests, when I finally awake after the early evening news.

So I trudge up the stairs, clutching a mug of cocoa and snuggle up in bed. I feel a bit more awake now, so I start to thumb through my share of the pony magazines that are lying invitingly on the floor shouting, *"Read me."*

I work my way down the pile, happily reading for hours. Finally, I reach the last magazine. I glance at the contents page, deciding what to read first (I'm a creature of habit, so it's usually the short story, followed by the helpful information articles). I'm starting to get sleepy, and, dreamily, I skim through the For Sale ads. The full color section is first, where a photo of the horse or pony being offered precedes each For Sale ad.

And then, out of the blue, I see her, staring up at me from the right hand page. She is the third *For Sale* ad.

I recognize the picture immediately. It is Snowstorm. *My* Snowstorm.

OK, so in reality, she *isn't* my pony and has *never* actually been *my* pony. But spiritually and emotionally, she belongs to me, and always will (It might sound heavy, but I'm sure you know what I mean...). Anyway, for a while, I just stare at the photograph of Snowstorm. I read the wording of the ad, over and over again:

Gray Welsh Section B mare, 13.2hh, nine years old, super jumper, bombproof. Quality pony, lovely temperament. Genuine reason for sale.

My eyes glaze over when I see the price, which is way over what I can afford. It will probably upset me, but I just know I have to see her. Then I remember that this is an old magazine. Trembling, I check the date – it is six months old! It is also nearly midnight – far too late to phone the

39

number. I will have to wait until morning, which is very frustrating. Not surprisingly, I now find it hard to sleep.

In the morning, I go straight around to see Ronnie. I say nothing but hand her the magazine and open to the page I have been studying so intensely.

She reads the ad, and then hands it back to me, her face full of concern. "But Matty, there's no way you can buy Snowstorm."

"I *know* that."

"Well, then. Anyway the ad is out of date, so if you do call, all it will do is make you unhappy. I know it's hard, but you really should leave it alone."

This is not what I want to hear, and not what I expect from Ronnie. She sounds very sleepy and I put down her negative response to feeling bad about what happened to poor Comfort.

Of course, I never do listen to advice, so the first thing I do when I get back is pick up the phone and dial the number. A girl's voice answers, cheerful and friendly.

"I saw your ad for the pony for sale –" I begin.

She interrupts quickly. "I think you must have made a mistake – that was months ago!"

"I know. I only just saw the ad," I try to explain. "But this pony is important to me. She was sold, you see, and I'm trying to trace her again –"

"Oh, she used to belong to you, did she?" the girl butts in again, but not rudely.

"Yes, that's right," I find myself lying.

"I see. Well, I'm sorry to have to tell you that she was sold really quickly, and as it was such a long time ago I'm afraid I didn't keep the details of where she went, except that it was somewhere in Wardely."

I tried to take this in, my hands shaking on the receiver. Wardely is miles away. "What did you expect, Matty?" I tell myself angrily. "Surely you didn't think that Snowstorm would still be for sale?"

The girl senses my upset.

"Look," she says kindly, "I'm so sorry to disappoint you. I know how hard it is to lose a pony. I didn't really want to sell her – she was the best pony I ever had, a real angel. But I suffer from asthma and unfortunately I developed an allergy to horses, so I had no choice. But please be assured she went to a very good home."

I get a sense of déja-vu, recalling Mark's words when he sold Snowstorm all that time ago.

"Thanks anyway," I murmur helplessly, ready to hang up.

"Wait," says the girl quickly, before I put the phone down. "Look, give me your phone number and if I can find anything about where she went, I'll let you know. I promise."

"I really would appreciate that," I say numbly. "Thanks again."

So, that was that. Suddenly, I am overwhelmed with a sense of sadness and loss, of the flame of hope briefly fanned but soon extinguished. I know I must try to put Snowstorm out of my mind. Somehow, though, hope never quite dies...

Time passes quickly and we are all relieved that Comfort seems to be recovering from her frightening experience in the swimming pool. Not being able to ride her again has been frustrating, but this is all part of the responsibilities of owning a pony. Finally, the vet agrees that she can be ridden once more, but lightly, with no galloping or jumping until she is completely fit.

Silke's arrival is imminent. The spare bed is made up in my room and Mom has decided that as Silke is the guest I should let her have my bed, so I am to have the cot. I can't say I'm too keen on this idea, as I like my own bed (see, I *am* selfish). We are due to collect her from the railway station at three o'clock. There is a direct connection from the airport, and Silke has traveled abroad before and seems fairly happy with this arrangement, which will save Dad having to battle with all the airport traffic.

As it is a Saturday, I am going to the stables as usual, but have agreed to come home early so there is plenty of time to get ready to go and get her with Dad. Of course, things don't go quite according to plan.

To start the day, when I call for Ronnie, her mom tells me that she has gotten tonsillitis and isn't allowed out, so I go to the Old Fort alone. I am disappointed, as I am looking forward to having a chat with Ronnie about Silke's impending visit. For some reason, I am apprehensive about it. It isn't logical, but there you are. On arrival at the stables, Gina announces that she has to go in an hour as her mom wants to take her shopping to choose some curtains, and Gina's opinion is essential. We both groan, but Gina generally gives in to her mom without a fight. So it is down to me and Spike to attend to our pony, who has now gotten into the habit of giving a little nicker of greeting when we arrive, which is lovely. She is turned out by day now, so we catch her, groom her and do her feet, and then take turns riding.

Spike goes first, and I sit on the fence and watch. Comfort's circles are getting much better now, not so shapeless and meandering. It has been raining and the field is a bit boggy, which makes it harder work for horse and rider. Unfortunately, I am wearing my jodhpur boots instead of long rubber boots, which would have been more sensible. They are soon caked in mud, which I transfer to the stirrups.

"That will be a nice cleaning job," remarks Spike, adding, "For you, Matty."

I pretend to hit her and she ducks. I accidentally catch poor Comfort on the nose. She is not amused and reacts by snorting and pushing me over backwards into the mud. Spike roars with laughter. It is the first time she has laughed in ages, so I can't be annoyed. I laugh too, but my jodhpurs are filthy, and my khaki sweater is a dirty brown. I can imagine Mom's face when I get home. I push a strand of wet hair off my face, leaving nice muddy streaks across my nose. Spike helps me up.

Although Comfort trots nicely around the school a couple of times, it has started to rain and she is getting a bit fed up by now, and starts to jog and shy. Spike tells me to reinforce my leg aids to keep her on the track, but I too have lost enthusiasm now that the rain is causing me to squish in the saddle.

We have just untacked and stabled Comfort when one of the working students appears and announces that Elliott has escaped again, and could we have all hands on deck to find him before he causes an accident? Finally we corner him in the top paddock, where he is standing innocently by the gate, his reins trailing, with a mischievous grin on his face. I wonder if we will have to chase him, but he waits meekly while we gather up the reins, apparently bored after his little adventure. We are leading him back when Spike says suddenly, "What time did you say you had to pick up Silke?"

I look at my watch and groan. It is already two o'clock. "I'm going to be late. Dad will be furious."

"Go on, you dash home. I'll take this devil back to the stables," she offers.

"Thanks, Spike, you're a pal," I tell her gratefully, feeling a wave of guilt again for even considering the financial difficulties her absence will cause us.

I run all the way but Dad is already waiting impatiently by the car.

"I'll just get changed –" I begin.

"No time for that, young lady. Come on, get in. The traffic will be bad enough as it is." His mood is not improved when, five minutes down the road, the car suddenly loses power and grinds to a halt.

"What's happened? Why have we stopped?" I ask, getting anxious. I have visions of Silke waiting on the station platform, forlorn and abandoned.

"It must be that dicey relay again. I meant to get it fixed, but I haven't had the time," explains Dad, getting out and lifting the hood. He fiddles around in the engine while I fiddle with my watch. Eventually he says, "I think you ought to make alternative arrangements to get to the station."

I almost say sarcastically, "And what might they be?" but decide against it. It will be expensive to get a taxi all the way to the station, but we are running out of time. Then my hero comes to the rescue. Just as all appears lost, a familiar four-wheel drive draws up beside us. It is Mark's dad, with Mark sitting beside him.

"Problems?"

Dad nods. "Breakdown. You couldn't do us a favor, could you? Run Matty to the station for me?"

Obligingly, Mark's dad agrees. "We were just about to visit that new music shop to look at another clarinet for Mark, but that can wait until later."

So I jump into the back of their big Range Rover and we manage to get to the station only ten minutes late.

At first, I think we have somehow missed Silke. There is only one female waiting on the platform, a tall, willowy blonde, with immaculate hair cut into the latest style, and tastefully applied eye make-up. From a distance, it doesn't look a bit like Silke. In the photo she had sent me, she had been wearing cut off jeans, Doc Martens and a striped T-shirt, her hair tied back with a rubber band. The girl on the platform is wearing black tights with a short stretchy black miniskirt, knee high black boots, a thin white sweater and an expensive looking leather jacket. Actually, she looks quite stunning and not at all what I expected.

"Matty?" she asks cautiously. She has seen my photo and clearly recognizes me instantly. Then she spots Mark.

"Matty, you didn't tell me you had a brother."

"Mark isn't my brother. He's my *boyfriend*," I reply, and for some reason there is an edge to my voice.

Mark gives a sheepish grin and Silke smiles back. For a moment, I cease to exist. Mark can't seem to take his eyes off her and for a moment I try to see it from Mark's viewpoint.

1. Me, with my short mousey brown hair, scruffy mud splattered sweater, filthy jodhpurs that are starting to smell a bit (yes, I did land in some manure when I fell over) and mud-streaked face.

2. Silke, with her blonde goddess looks and tasteful clothes.

I'll go over that again.

1. Me

2. Silke.

Let's see now, if you were a boy, which would you choose? Something told me that Silke's visit was not getting off to a good start.

Chapter 4

So that Silke doesn't get her chic clothes messed up by brushing against the clods of mud on my jodhpurs and boots, Mark's dad suggests that she sit in the back of the car, next to Mark. I feel like the outcast, on my own in the passenger seat, and to make matters worse it is hard for me to join in any conversation without constantly craning my neck around at an uncomfortable angle. Still, Mark and Silke don't seem that interested in what I have to say, so finally I give up and sulk, and resort to picking and flicking bits of dried mud off my boots until there is a little pile on the floor under my seat. Mark's dad seems not to notice. Perhaps he, too, is captivated by the wondrous Silke. Hey, I don't sound that jealous, do I? OK, so the fact that I discover that Mark can speak some German (he's in a higher year than me at school, and much brainier) is even more irritating, meaning that he and Silke can mumble and giggle together without me understanding a word. She has a delicate, charming laugh, somehow, and acts in a way that makes her seem older than she is. In fact, she is actually only one year older than I.

I am relieved when the journey is over. Mark, ever the gentleman, offers to carry Silke's rather large suitcase into our house, while Mom hovers and fusses and thanks Mark's dad for helping out. The suitcase is actually far too heavy for Mark (what has she got in it?) but, being a boy, he won't admit it. I can't help smiling to myself as he puffs and heaves it up the stairs to my room.

"I have to get back to the stables, now," Mark's dad explains when Mom offers everyone lemonade. "But thanks, anyway. There isn't time to go and look at that clarinet now, I'm afraid," he says to Mark.

"That's OK," shrugs Mark. "We can do it some other time. I'll make my own way back home."

"Oh, you play clarinet, too?" asks Silke, whose English is impeccable, with only the faintest trace of accent. "You must be very talented."

"Oh, he is," agrees Mom. "He plays in a jazz band. With Matty's dad."

I don't think Silke hears that last bit. She is too busy concentrating on Mark.

Just then, Dad comes in, complaining that the car has developed more than one fault, and the garage can't fix the car for a week, and what has happened to old-fashioned service? Then he spots Silke, and gives her a welcoming smile.

"I'm so sorry you had to wait," he says, explaining what happened. "I hope you weren't getting worried."

Silke smiles. "I am used to traveling. I have been to America before, and to India on my own. Of course, I stayed with friends when I arrived. Traveling is so exciting, don't you think?"

"I imagine so," Dad replies. Neither of my parents have traveled outside the country and Silke regales them with stories of how her luggage got lost in Delhi and how she came face to face with a mountain lion when trail riding in the Rockies. Trail riding... Well, at least we were getting nearer to a conversation I can get enthusiastic about.

"That sounds like fun," I say. "What was your pony like?"

"Oh, I can't remember exactly, gray, I think. But the views were breathtaking, and the scenery..."

Views? Scenery? What about the horses? How could she not remember what her pony was like? This is not boding well. I try again.

"Surely, you must remember? How long were you riding for? A day? A week?"

But Silke appears not to have heard me, and they are already onto the next topic of conversation, which seems to revolve around the huge helpings of food you get in American restaurants. I am about to give up and go and have a bath when Silke says, "Would you mind very much if I have a shower? It was a long journey, and I really would like to freshen up."

"Of course, dear, I'll get some towels for you. I did some washing earlier, but there's enough hot water for one more shower."

When Silke and Mom have left the room, Dad says, "What a lovely girl. So polite and well mannered." Then he frowns across at me, wrinkles his nose and says, "God, Matty, are you still wearing those smelly jodhpurs? They stink of horse manure."

At which point Mark thanks us for the lemonade and gets up to go.

"I'll walk back with you," I offer.

"Matty, where are your manners?" chides Dad. "Silke is your guest and you want to abandon her as soon as she has arrived."

52

Actually I would very much liked to have abandoned her. Instead, I protest, "I'm hardly stranding her, am I? You and Mom are here, and she'll probably be hours in the bathroom."

But Dad won't hear of it and Mark doesn't exactly fight in my corner, so I have to give in.

Silke is indeed hours in the shower (one and a half, to be precise). My clothes feel as if they are welded to my body and no one wants to sit near me. Finally, she emerges from the bathroom, wrapped in a white fluffy bathrobe, with a towel wrapped around her head like a yellow turban. She gives me a dazzling smile and says, "I hope I have not taken too much time in your bathroom."

I try not to show my annoyance – after all, she is the guest. Sensing my irritation, and wanting to repair any damage, she adds, "We can have a nice chat later on, OK?"

I nod and smile back. Perhaps things will get better after all. Perhaps I am pre-judging her. I look forward to soaking in a hot bath with the soothing herbal bath oil Mom got me for Christmas, forgetting that all the hot water has been used up. Cursing, I have a hasty dip in lukewarm water. I can't face washing my hair in cold water, so I pull a comb through it, change into a clean sweatshirt and jeans and join Silke and my parents for an early supper.

I had been hoping to take Silke to the stables to introduce her to Comfort, but it is too dark by now so I decide to do this the next morning.

"I hope you like your room, Silke," says Mom anxiously.

"Thank you, it is very sweet," Silke replies politely.

I squirm inwardly. Firstly it is *my* room, not Silke's. OK, so she has been given my bed. But this is a temporary arrangement. Secondly, she describes my room as *sweet*? Untidy, perhaps (although Mom made me tidy up for Silke, it still isn't exactly immaculate). She makes it sound as if I have alphabet wallpaper and cuddly toys. How can you call posters of horses and ponies on every available surface sweet? I wonder what her room is like.

Just before we go to bed, the phone rings. I answer and am pleased that it is Mark.

"How is Silke settling in?" he asks and suddenly I am not so pleased.

"Fine," I reply curtly.

"Good. Dad and I want to invite her – and you, of course – to lunch tomorrow. What do you think?"

"Great," I reply. But for some reason, I don't feel as pleased as I sound.

"Good. I won't chat. I promised to help Dad out with

some paperwork before we turn in. See you tomorrow then, about one."

I tell Silke and she is obviously delighted.

"You are very lucky, Matty, to have such a great boyfriend," she says.

"Very lucky," agrees Mom, and I am sure she is mentally comparing my jeans with Silke's smart velvet leggings and chenille sweater.

I don't find the cot very comfortable, but Silke looks snug and content in my lovely bed and thick comforter. I ask her questions about her home and family, and the pony she looked after for a friend, and her trail riding, but she answers in monosyllables, so our promised chat does not materialize. Before long, I hear her snoring gently. At least she isn't so perfect, I conclude, smiling to myself.

The next morning I am up and alert for once, and by eight thirty am ready to take Silke to the stables. But despite my usual banging and crashing around the bedroom as I try to find the clothes I hurled onto the floor the night before (in contrast to Silke's neatly folded clothes placed carefully over the chair) I fail to disturb her in the least.

The sun is shining for once, and I am eager to ride.

At nine o' clock, I am about to wake her but Mom says in shocked tones, "Really, Matty, she is our guest. She must be tired. Let her sleep."

"OK," I reply. "I'll go to the stables and come back for her later."

Mom looks disapproving. "You can't do that. You should be looking after her, not abandoning her. No, Matty, you invited her here, so you must wait until she wakes and then ask what she wants to do."

"But, Mom!" My protests fall on deaf ears. This is not turning out the way I imagined at all.

Silke finally stirs at eleven thirty. By the time she has showered (again), and washed her hair (again) it is nearly lunchtime. I want to scream.

"I thought you might like to come and see my pony," I say to her, pulling my long rubber boots on while she is draining the last dregs of her juice.

"That would be nice, Matty, but I thought we were going to have lunch at Mark's house soon. Will there be time?"

I groan. I had already forgotten about our lunch invitation. "Darn, so we are."

"You don't sound very pleased," Silke observes. "I thought Mark was your boyfriend."

"He is. I just forgot, that's all, and I didn't realize it was so late."

"You must try to be better organized, Matty," says Mom, and I wonder who to strangle first – my annoying visitor or my infuriating Mom.

We take the bus over to Mark's house and I notice that several of the boys sitting at the back are looking at Silke. She is wearing her black velvet leggings again, with high-heeled suede ankle boots and her leather jacket. I am wearing my khaki combat trousers and brown trail jacket. An interesting combination, you might think. But not exactly a fashion statement. Still, I intend to zoom over to the stables as soon as lunch is over.

Mark greets us with a silly grin on his face. When the meal is over, Mark's dad apologizes and says he has to go over to the stables.

"I was going to take Silke to see Comfort, so we could join you," I venture.

At last.

I have noticed the sun getting duller as the day has gone on and expect rain at any time. But to my horror, Mark says, "Maybe we could go over later, Matty? There's plenty of time to visit the stables, and I want to play Silke a tune I've written for the clarinet. If that's OK," he adds, noticing my obvious disappointment. I feel unable to protest.

Mark has never played me any of his compositions. But then, I suppose I never showed the interest in his music that Silke seems to. Apparently, Silke plays the piano, so she can read music, which gives them another thing in common.

An hour drags by. Then another. I wander outside and gaze across the horizon. I imagine Spike and Gina trying to persuade Comfort to trot in a circle without cutting the corners. I hope they won't be mad that I am not there to help them.

A spit of rain hits my nose, then another and another, and within minutes it is pouring down. Back inside, Mark and Silke hardly seem to have moved from the sofa, where they are absorbed in conversation, this time about the merits of jazz music as opposed to classical. I stifle a yawn.

"Come on, you two. If we don't get to the stable soon, it will be getting too dark to ride."

Mark looks up apologetically. "Sorry Matty. We forgot. I'll just get my jacket."

"Oh, is it raining?" Silke appears to have only just noticed the downpour beating against the window.

"Just a bit," I reply.

She looks down at her fashionable boots. "If we have to walk over fields, these will be ruined. They are quite expensive."

"Oh, dear. We mustn't have that," says Mark. "You can borrow some of my boots, if you like."

I try not to giggle as I picture the elegant Silke in green boots.

Silke smiles sweetly. "Thank you, Mark that is very kind. But I have rather small feet. I don't think any of your boots would fit me."

"You could always stuff newspaper inside them," I suggest.

"Don't be daft, Matty," says Mark. "We'll just have to wait for a bit longer. I don't expect the rain will last."

Of course, it does. Two hours pass. Then it gets dark. It is still raining when Mark's dad returns, so he offers to drive us back home. Mom and Dad are watching TV when we get back.

"Oh, by the way, Matty, Spike and Gina came by earlier. I told them you were out for the day. They looked a bit miffed."

Great. My friends are annoyed with me and I have

gone a whole day without seeing my pony. I think I am being very tolerant. But how will I survive three weeks of this?

I decide to sneak next door and see how Ronnie is feeling. Of course, the real reason is that I want some sympathy. Her mother, who answers the door, sounds harassed.

"Do come in, Matty. I'm sure Ronnie will be pleased to see you. She's a bit miserable at the moment."

Kirk and Douglas, Ronnie's twin four-year-old brothers, are wailing and arguing over their toys and generally making lots of noise, so I am not surprised that Ronnie is fed up. I go up to her bedroom and pour out my tale of woe, the disaster on the way to collect Silke, and how she looks terrific and is health conscious, but doesn't really seem into ponies in the way I had expected. Then I regale her with my boring day at Mark's.

"Poor you," she says sympathetically, as I expected. Her voice is more of a whisper and she says it is painful to swallow. Even so, we talk for ages about all sorts of things, mostly horse-related.

"Mark's dad really has restored the Old Fort to its former glory," I observe.

"Yes, it was wasteland before he took it over," Ronnie agrees.

I remembered the first time we went there. It was huge, and derelict, with graying, crumbling bricks and overgrown with weeds. We had kept Moonlight there in secret for a while, since we had nowhere else to go. It was supposed to be haunted, according to Spike, by Mad Major Wilkins who jumped his horse over the edge of the quarry during a terrible storm. Horse and rider had perished horribly. I never knew for sure whether or not she was making it up, but the fort was always a bit eerie at night.

"When I'm old enough to leave home, I want to live somewhere warm," says Ronnie suddenly. "Perhaps Southern Italy. I'll have a huge white walled villa and a charming stable block and keep Andalusian horses."

I laugh. "So what happened to your chain of vegetarian restaurants idea?"

"Oh, that. Well, I'll go to Italy *after* I've run the restaurants, and they will have been so hugely successful that I will have sold them off to finance my new home in Italy," she explains convincingly.

I am feeling quite relaxed until Ronnie's mom suddenly pokes her head around the door.

"Matty, dear, your mom has just phoned – she says can you please go back home at once, because you are neglecting your guest!"

Chapter 5

When I wake up the next morning, I make a decision. I am going to the stables to see Comfort and to heck with what anyone else says. I can tackle Mom and Dad when I get back. I am not having my vacation spoiled like this.

I peer over at Silke and she is snoring gently as usual. Even when she is sleeping her hair looks pretty, as if it had been specially arranged on the pillow, like one of those glossy photos of models you get in women's magazines.

I shower, dress and sneak downstairs for juice and toast. It is only seven thirty. Mom and Dad are still asleep, both having taken the week off from work to relax and concentrate on gardening (Mom) and golf (Dad). It's quite peaceful sitting on my own while eating and looking out into our little yard. The sun is shining, and for once it looks as if the weather might be on my side. I decide that I will concentrate on Comfort's transitions this morning, particularly trot to halt. That will stop Mark from being so smug. Sometimes I think it is such a waste, a talented rider who no longer rides. Still, he does love his music, and it must have been nice for him to share his interest with Silke, even though it irritated me. Perhaps I should try to show more of an interest, find out more about music. I'm sure Mark would appreciate that. Perhaps I should learn an instrument? It sounds fine in theory, but in practice, when would I find the time? Anyway, I am a slow learner. I am turning these thoughts over in my mind when a sweet-toned voice says, "Can I join you for breakfast?"

I am shocked. It is Silke. She must have moved fast (and quietly). She is already dressed, this time in clean designer jeans and a smart black polo neck sweater.

"Yes, help yourself," I reply, my mouth still full of half chewed toast. I had not expected this.

"I know you have been dying to see your pony, and I feel bad that because of me you have not done so," she continues. "So I am up bright and early and ready to go." She gives me a big, radiant smile.

"Great," I reply, still reeling from the shock.

On the way to the stables, we chat properly for the first time, and I learn more about Silke's family and home. Her Mom is a marketing consultant and her dad is a political journalist. I gather that they are both away on business much of the time.

"But you get used to being on your own and having to look after yourself," Silke comments, a little sadly. "I am very independent. And Klaus, my older brother, and I get on really well so we keep each other company. But now that he has gone to art school, I do miss him. He's really my best friend. If only I hadn't..."

She stops suddenly and I notice she looks upset about something. Then, with an effort, her voice brightens again. "Anyway, Matty, tell me all about your friends."

By the time we arrive at the Old Fort I have given Silke an abridged history, including Miss Pugh, Mark's dad saving the ponies, and of course, our adventures with Moonlight. Gina and Spike are already there, and I wonder what my friends will think of Silke.

Spike looks up from the wheelbarrow of straw and manure that she is taking to the muckheap.

"Good timing, Matty. We've just finished mucking out," she says with an edge to her voice. I recall what

Mom said yesterday, about them being miffed to think I was out all day and shirking my share of the work.

Gina smiles, trying to lighten the atmosphere. "Hi, Matty, we wondered where you were. We thought you would be here yesterday."

I find myself blushing, wanting to explain, but not wanting to blame Silke when she is standing beside me. However, Silke senses the problem and says, "I am afraid that is my fault. Matty was stuck looking after me for the day. By the way, I am Silke." She has such a winning smile, and I am grateful to her for explaining.

"Nice to meet you, Silke," says Gina. "So you're Matty's pen pal. How do you like it here?"

"I have been made very welcome," Silke replies.

Spike, however, doesn't look very welcoming. In fact she looks positively grumpy, and I wonder if she has been arguing again with her parents. Gina shoots me a warning glance, as if to tell me to be careful what I say to her.

"I thought I would bring Silke along to see our pony," I explain. "And," I add hastily, "To do my share of the work."

Spike is not pacified and wanders off without speaking.

"She had a fight with her dad, about the move," Gina whispers when Spike is out of earshot. "I'm sure she'll be more friendly later on."

We introduce Silke to our pony, who seems to have

caught Spike's mood and is sulking in the corner of the stable, resting a hind leg, head hanging down, not at all friendly.

"She was a bit of a pain yesterday," explains Gina. "Spike took her out for a trail ride, or rather, tried to, but Comfort shied when a blackbird flew out of the hedge by the gate, and Spike went flying over her head and bruised her arm."

"Spike doesn't usually get taken by surprise like that," I observe.

Gina shrugged. "I guess Spike was in the wrong kind of mood, because she didn't bother to get back on, but just gave up and put Comfort back in the stable. I didn't like my chances, not without Spike, so it wasn't a very productive day."

"We have to get Comfort used to trail riding," I insist. "She will never earn her keep as a working boarder at this rate." I can see an impending cash flow disaster looming if we don't sort Comfort out.

"We could take her out for a trail ride today," I suggest. "After all, there are three of us. (I am including Silke, not Spike.) "Safety in numbers, and if I ride, and you, Gina, and Silke walk on either side of her, that should make Comfort feel safer."

Silke doesn't look too keen on this idea. "If your pony is dangerous –" she begins.

"Goodness, Comfort isn't dangerous," I reply. "She's just nervous about roads and traffic, and who can blame her for that? We're trying to re-school her, but it's a bit of an uphill struggle. Would you mind, just walking out with us?"

There is a long pause and I wonder what I should do. If Silke doesn't want to join us, we would have to leave her alone at the stables where she doesn't know anyone, which doesn't seem very fair. However, I really want to ride Comfort...

Then, at that very moment, Mark appears. My savior!

"Hi, girls," he says cheerily. "Where's Dad? I'm due to meet him here. We're going into town, to try and get this new clarinet, since we didn't make it on Saturday."

I smile. He had postponed his new clarinet to help me get Silke. And now I am about to ask him for another favor, one I am sure he will be happy to oblige.

"Mark," I begin.

"Yes, Matty. What do you want this time? I recognize your begging voice."

"Slight problem," I say, grabbing his arm and pulling him out of earshot. "I really must take Comfort out today, but I don't think Silke wants to come and I can't abandon her, so..."

"So you want me to look after her for the day, is that it?"

"You've got it," I nod. "I'm sure she would love to go into town with you."

"OK. I'll ask her," and he turns to Silke and says, "How would you like spending the morning with me? I could show you the shops, we could have some lunch... what do you think?"

Silke doesn't even try to disguise her delight at the idea, her radiant smile bigger than ever. "That would be wonderful. Oh, but Matty, I hope you won't mind."

"Mind? Of course not. We've got three weeks together, so we'll have plenty of time to do things, and this way I can still ride Comfort."

With everything settled, I can concentrate on my pony without worrying about Silke. It is the perfect solution. So why do I feel uneasy as I watch Silke walk away arm in arm with Mark?

However, I soon put this out of my mind as Gina and I give Comfort a thorough brushing before we tack her up. She is still scowling when we set off down the lane, Gina at her head, ready to grab the reins at the slightest provocation.

It is not an easy ride. We take the quietest route, sticking to fields initially, and then risking the side roads on the edge of the housing estates. I ride on the grass verges where possible, and we stay at walk throughout, risking trot only occasionally. I have to be on constant alert, since Comfort shies at every opportunity. It is a terrible habit, and I wonder if her last owner knew about it. Would we have bought her, had we known? If we had been more knowledgeable, or cautious, I could be riding a completely different pony at this moment in time. We might even have been taking prizes at the local show. It's hard to imagine winning anything on Comfort.

Throughout the forty-five minute ride Comfort shies at (in order of occurrence):

A tree

An abandoned microwave oven at the dump

The dump in general (a great source of alarm)

An empty potato chip packet on the path

Two sparrows having a dust bath in the road

A garden gate with squeaky hinges

A large Labrador dog barking behind the gate (admittedly, he was a bit fierce)

A plastic gnome in the same garden

Derek, the postman

A parked car

Gina's dangly earrings

The tree again (which we passed on the return to the stables)

I ask if Gina wants to swap halfway through the ride,

but she sensibly declines. When we return, my arms feel as if they have been pulled out of their sockets, with all the constant squeezing and pulling on the reins.

I feel a surge of relief as I dismount. Since my arms are no longer functioning normally, Gina kindly untacks Comfort and rubs her down before turning her out in the field with the other ponies. We resolve to recommence Comfort's schooling later on.

Since Gina and I are both shattered by now, we decide to walk back to my place, which is nearest, and dig out some of my books on schooling ponies to see if we can locate something that might be helpful. Mom is in the kitchen, loading the dishwasher, and says, "There was a phone call for you earlier, Matty. A girl. She left her number."

"Right." I wonder vaguely who it could have been. Mom knows the voices of most of my friends and she would have said if it was anyone familiar. I dial the number and instantly recognize the voice.

"Hello, you called me a while ago about a pony I sold?"

"Yes." My heart begins to thump. She must have some news on Snowstorm!

"Well, after a lot of digging around I finally found the telephone number of the lady I sold her to. So, have you got a pen?"

In my excitement I fumble madly, but of course there are no writing tools of any description on the little table that houses the phone, and my pockets are no use.

"Mom, pen, pen!" I shout rudely. Grunting at my lack of manners Mom does, however, produce a pen that works.

"Got one," I gasp, my hand shaking as she reads the number. The area code sounds vaguely familiar, and I realize with mounting excitement that it's not too far away.

"Well, good luck," says the girl warmly. "I hope you find her."

"Thank you. I hope so, too," I reply.

For a moment I just stand looking at the phone number, unable to believe that this is happening. I have visions of Snowstorm, galloping to greet me, and am filled with anticipation. But, somewhere, at the back of my mind, is an unaccountable premonition of fear.

Chapter 6

Gina and I decide to visit Ronnie to give her this latest revelation and also update her on progress with Comfort.

She is in bed, propped up on pillows.

"I can't speak properly," Ronnie explains in a wispy voice. "It hurts when I talk. It feels like I've swallowed a set of golf balls and a roll of sandpaper at one sitting."

"Poor Ronnie," says Gina sympathetically. "We can do the talking for you."

I tell them both about the phone call I have just received, and that there now seems real hope of locating Snowstorm.

"I understand how you feel, but this is a mission of madness," remarks Gina. "After all, you don't have the money to buy her back."

"I've told her that," rasps Ronnie. "But you know Matty. Nothing stops her once she's made her mind up."

There is an awkward silence. Gina, tactfully, decides to change the subject.

"So, Ronnie, when will you be back in action?"

Ronnie groans. "Another week at least. Sorry to abandon you all with the demon pony."

"Oh, don't worry about that," laughs Gina. "We're saving up all the mucking out, just for you!"

"I can't wait," Ronnie giggles hoarsely. "So, Matty, how are things going with Silke now?"

I shrug. "Better, I think. We had a bit of a chat today."

"She seems nice enough," comments Gina. "And she is very pretty. But if I were you, Matty, with Silke around, I would watch your boyfriend. Because Mark is certainly interested in her."

I try to laugh this off, but I can't help feeling that she has a point.

I get back just before Silke and Mark return.

"It was so kind of Mark to take me out," gushes Silke. She seems to have acquired a number of shopping bags from the more expensive clothing stores in town. "I had a lovely time."

"My pleasure," replies Mark, and I notice that they seem to be looking at each other quite a bit. Or perhaps I am imagining this?

"Silke asked me if there were any good dance clubs

around here, as she really likes dancing," Mark says, helping Silke with her bags.

"Tough luck," I laugh. There isn't much at all to do locally, apart from the burger joint and movie house. There is only one nightclub, which I had heard was expensive. Not only that, you have to be eighteen to get in.

"That's what I said," agrees Mark. "So I've decided to throw a party on Saturday. We can show Silke that we know how to have a good time around here."

I am a little surprised at this, but Mark is bubbling over with enthusiasm.

"There's lots of room at my house. We can invite people from the stables and the jazz group and school..."

"Sounds terrific," beams Silke.

"Yeah, great," I add, recalling Gina's earlier remark and feeling uneasy.

When Mark has gone, Silke asks me if I had a good ride on Comfort, but before I can answer she starts to unload her shopping bags to show me what she has bought: a gorgeous sleeveless silk dress the color of poppies; a long scarf to match her sweater; two very short lycra skirts, both black, and a pair of ethnic bead earrings.

"And this is for you," she says triumphantly, just when I have been consumed with envy at the money she must have.

74

She produces a huge, lavishly illustrated encyclopaedia of horses. It is quite magnificent and very expensive. I am consumed with guilt at every negative thought I have ever had about Silke since her arrival.

"Do you like it?" she asks, sounding anxious.

"It's wonderful. I love it. You shouldn't have," I add hastily, thinking, "But I'm so glad you have!"

During tea, she gives Mom a book on cultivating roses and Dad a video on playing golf. They are delighted, and her position in the household is assured.

While they are all absorbed in conversation in the living room, I sneak out to make a phone call. I'm sure you will guess who I intend to phone. After all, I never listen to anyone's advice, or so Mom keeps telling me. I am headstrong and impetuous, Dad says, and it will be my downfall. Even so...

The phone rings and rings and I am just about to hang up when a woman answers.

"I'm enquiring about a pony I believe you bought about six months ago," I begin nervously. "A Welsh mare, gray, 13.2 hands high –"

"Oh, the one we have for sale? Did you see the ad in the evening paper? We've had half a dozen calls already," she replies airily.

So, Snowstorm is for sale *again*? I check through

some details with her to ensure we are talking about the same pony.

"It's my daughter's pony. A really super animal. Sadly, we have to sell. We are moving to New Zealand shortly and we can't take the pony with us."

She chatters on about their new house in New Zealand, and her husband's job, which is of no interest to me whatsoever. I listen politely, and finally she says, "You are aware of the asking price?"

"Money is not a problem," I lie. Of course, I have no idea of the asking price but this does not deter me. Snowstorm is *available*. It is a dream come true (apart from the minor issue that I have no funds to speak of).

And before I hang up I have arranged to view Snowstorm the following afternoon at 4 pm. I decide not to tell anyone about this. I will go alone.

Snowstorm's current home is miles away, out in the middle of the countryside, and not on a bus route. This presents me with a problem. If I don't tell anyone what I'm doing, I can't ask Dad for a lift there, and I can't afford a taxi. So I make another rash and, in retrospect, foolish decision on the spur of the moment. I decide to ride there on Comfort.

Luckily, the next day, Silke offers to help Mom in the

garden, so I don't have the additional problem of what to do with her while I sneak off to see Snowstorm. As you may gather, I am doing all the wrong things and setting myself up for disaster.

1. I am riding on an unreliable pony who hates traffic.
2. I am going alone.
3. I am not telling anyone where I am going.

Be warned. Do not do this yourself.

I reckon it will take me three hours to get there, but just in case, I decide to leave the stables by 12:30 at the latest. I have some directions, and the route sounds pretty straightforward. I spend the early morning with Gina and Spike, doing the usual chores, and watch while Gina (reluctantly) schools Comfort in the ring, under Spike's watchful eye. They actually have a good session, with Comfort managing the trot to halt transition for the first time ever without poking her nose in the air. In fact, flushed by success, Gina attempts a halt to canter transition, but this is far too advanced and difficult for Comfort to grasp and she gets confused and bucks. Luckily, Gina is prepared and keeps her seat. We give her a round of applause and, while she is grinning at us, Comfort gives another buck and sends her flying.

We insist that Gina gets back on, to her annoyance, and do some more walking and trotting before giving in. Then we stable Comfort and get ready for lunch. I am so nervous at the impending secret visit to see Snowstorm that I'm unable to eat, so I leave Gina and Spike munching sandwiches in the indoor ring while I fetch Comfort's tack and prepare to go. It is nearly 12:15.

Comfort glares at me in disgust when she sees the bridle over my arm. She had thought her work was done for the day.

"Sorry to disappoint you," I tell her in conciliatory tones. I even offer her the bribe of a polo mint to open her mouth to let me put the bit in. When I lower the saddle she gives a huge sigh.

"Poor thing," I commiserate. When I pull the girth tight, I discover it is impossible to pull to its usual position. She really is getting fat. "I think you should go on a diet," I tell her. She scowls.

After making me hop about in the stirrup a few times, finally Comfort lets me mount properly, and once I have adjusted the stirrup leathers (my legs are much shorter than Gina's) we are off.

I have decided to take the route via the back roads, which

I hope will be fairly quiet. It will take longer than going across country, but I have allowed extra time. On the last part of the journey, however, I realize we will have to cut across farmland to get to Snowstorm's new address. I pray we don't meet a tractor. Still, we will cross that bridge when we come to it, so to speak.

I am getting used to being constantly alert with Comfort shying at the silliest things, and it doesn't worry me like it used to. It's just a nuisance. I think of Snowstorm, of her perfect transitions and fluid paces. Compared to Comfort... Then I feel guilty. It is not productive to make comparisons between one pony and another, Ronnie has pointed out to me in the past, and quite rightly so. I am an ungrateful brat. I know plenty of people who would give anything to have a pony like Comfort – or any pony, for that matter. And here I am, riding the pony I part-own with my three closest friends. I am very lucky.

   It was just as silly to compare myself to Silke. After all, how would I like it if Mark kept saying how much prettier than I she was, and how much smarter? I wouldn't like it at all. Of course, Mark would never say such things. But I begin to wonder if he *thinks* them...

I am starting to turn this over in my mind, and for a

brief spell of time, perhaps less than a minute, I lose concentration. So, at first, I am not aware of the idiot on a racing bike who comes whizzing around the corner on the wrong side of the road until it is too late to take avoiding action.

He just seems to appear from nowhere around a blind bend. Clearly he is just as surprised to see us, not expecting a pony to be trotting on the road. He is going too fast, (he later admits this) and in an effort to avoid us, he brakes violently, skids and goes flying over the handlebars of his expensive racing bike. Comfort is rooted to the spot, eyes goggling, too frightened to move. It is as if in an instant all her worse fears about being ridden outside the safety of the riding school are coming true. All her shying and nerves have been justified. Too late, I haul on her mouth, and she does a little pirouette but is still directly in the path of the bike, which just keeps coming. As soon as the cycle wheel makes contact with her shoulder, she rears up into the air and I, not surprisingly, end up on the grass verge, landing not far from the cyclist.

I am terrified that she will bolt off into the road, but after the impact Comfort just stands there, shocked and dazed, her head hanging and blood trickling down her knees, forming a little pool on the road. I feel sick.

"Are you alright?" asks the biker, trying to stand up. "I'm so sorry. I was going too fast – it was entirely my fault."

I nod and get on my feet, my legs shaking. My shoulder hurts and my knee is throbbing but I rush to Comfort to administer first aid.

"Easy, girl," I whisper, trying to soothe her. The bleeding looks bad and I tear the sleeves off my cotton shirt to make a bandage. She is shivering now and I am concerned she will go into shock. I start to panic.

"There's a call box down the road," says the cyclist, who has been unable to stand. "I would offer to get help, but my ankle is twisted or something, and I can't put any weight on it." He winces with pain at this last re-mark and I notice that his face is very pale.

Since his bike is a now a crumpled heap and he is unable to walk, it is up to me to set off on foot for help. I loop the reins around his arm and he offers to keep an eye on Comfort while I run to call for a vet.

It seems to take an age to reach the call box. My legs feel like lead and it is as if I am living a nightmare. As I dial for the vet and then an ambulance, all thoughts of Snowstorm are momentarily forgotten.

I go back and wait with the cyclist, who keeps repeating

how sorry he is and how he will never forgive himself if Comfort dies.

"She won't die," I snap, holding Comfort and trying to soothe her. She is trembling and shivering.

I begin to feel sick. I should never have brought her out on the road in the first place. My desire to see Snowstorm again has overtaken any common sense I had left.

"You don't deserve to have *any* pony, Matty Mathews," a little voice inside my head admonishes.

Eventually, after what seems like hours, but is in fact less than ten minutes, emergency help arrives.

Chapter 7

"You're very lucky, girls. *Very* lucky. The outcome could have been *much* worse." The vet gives Comfort a final pat before closing the stable door. We are back at the Old Fort, where Comfort has been brought home after undergoing a number of tests and x-rays. His words echo in my head as I relive the last few hours.

Comfort had walked meekly with me into the vet's horse trailer after our wait at the roadside, and we had set off for the animal hospital. The ambulance had already taken the cyclist away with a suspected broken ankle.

And now we are all gathered around Comfort – me, Spike and Gina – and I hardly dare face them. After all, I should never have taken Comfort out alone. She wasn't ready. How would she ever be able to trust us again?

If it had been the other way around, if it was Spike, or Gina, for instance, who had taken Comfort out, I would have felt as angry with them as I do with myself right now.

"Don't worry, Matty, we don't blame you," says Gina, seeing my concern.

"No, not *entirely*," adds Spike. "But you shouldn't have –"

"I know," I cut her off sharply. "You don't need to say it. I know."

"Please, let's not argue," urges Gina. "The main thing is that Comfort is going to be all right. She's had a bad shock, but her shoulder will heal; the wounds were not deep. Like the vet says, it could have been a lot worse."

"It certainly could," the vet agrees. "After all, she could have lost the foal."

"Excuse me?" I must have misheard him. "What foal are we talking about?"

The vet looks impatient. "A pregnant mare should not be subjected to excessive excitement, and certainly not a trauma like this."

Spike looks puzzled, and Gina's mouth drops open

"Are you saying that Comfort is pregnant?" I ask, my voice shaking.

The vet sighs. "Yes. She's due in seven months."

"I don't believe it," mutters Gina, shaking her head in a daze.

"She can't be," adds Spike.

"We did think Comfort seemed to be putting on weight," I burble, blushing furiously. Suddenly, Gina starts to giggle and, one by one, we all join in. It is a much-needed release of tension. Only when we have become hysterical does the vet rein us in, so to speak.

"Now, back to more serious issues," he says, his voice changing. "Comfort will need a lot of care. Take it easy for now, but in a few months time, no more riding. Thank goodness you hadn't been doing anything like cross country jumping or hill riding." There was a pause. "*Have* you?"

"We should be so lucky," mumbled Spike. "Getting her to trot is an effort."

"Good," replies the vet. "I'll give you a diet sheet, to make sure she gets the right vitamins and minerals. She can carry on living outside – the fresh air and exercise will do her good – but bring her in for an evening feed and hay net. You don't need to groom her every day – she needs some grease in her coat to protect her if the weather is bad. A brush once or twice a week to get rid of dried mud and matted hair should be enough. Her feet are OK and she's been wormed. I'll come back in a couple of days to check that she hasn't picked up any infections in those wounds. Otherwise, it should be clear sailing. See you soon, girls."

With that, he climbs into his four-wheel drive, and I am sure I hear him laughing softly to himself. I hardly dare look at the bill he has handed me. Perhaps the vet should take up permanent residence at the Old Fort?

"Well, this sure is one for the books," says Gina. "I still can't believe it."

"How could it have happened?" wonders Spike.

A thought occurs to me. "It must have been when she got out and went missing for two days earlier in the year. Remember? When Elliott decided to make a bid for freedom and we found him at the Garden Center and Comfort wandering in that field by the woods. I wonder where she could have met other horses?"

Gina giggles. "She may have romanced a prize stallion, a champion Thoroughbred. We may have a super little foal."

"Well, we won't even have a clue until he or she is born," I respond. "Perhaps we will never know. Perhaps it will forever remain another unsolved mystery!"

"Whatever the situation, from now on, we had better make sure that we take extra good care of Comfort, our little mother-to-be. No escaping from fields or encounters with cyclists or swimming pools," says Gina.

I notice Spike looking at me. She is still angry. "Matty, what were you doing taking her out on your own like that? Why didn't you tell us?" she demands.

At first, I try to make excuses, but then I realize I have to admit to the truth. "I was going to see Snowstorm. I didn't want anyone to know."

"But why keep it a secret? I thought you trusted us."

"It wasn't that, Spike. It's just that you all said I shouldn't go. If I had told you, you would have tried to talk me out of it. You would think I was being silly."

"Too right," agrees Spike. "What you did was unforgivable."

"Stop it, you two," shouts Gina. "I think we have all had enough for today. I don't know about you, but I could do with some water. I've still got some left in my bottle. Do you want to join me or not?"

Well, we all stay at the stables until it gets dark and Mark's dad finally convinces us that Comfort will be fine, but that if anything bad happens he will call us immediately. We agree to show up first thing the next morning. I have been so worried about Comfort that missing my appointment to see Snowstorm has taken a back seat for the time being. But now that I'm sure Comfort is safe, I decide to call Snowstorm's owners to explain what has happened. Perhaps I can rearrange to see her tomorrow.

But when I phone the number again, I get an unexpected shock.

"Sorry, dear," the woman says curtly. "I'm afraid the pony has been sold. She's already gone."

My stomach does a somersault. "Perhaps you would be kind enough to tell me where she has gone." My voice is quaking.

"Oh, I couldn't possibly do that. I can't disclose the new owner's address. That would be most unprofessional."

"But I really have to –"

"That is the end of the matter." And with that, she hangs up on me.

In deep despair, I go to see Ronnie. I need a shoulder to cry on. I tell her everything. Understandably her concern is for Comfort and it takes a lot of reassurance from me to satisfy her that our pony will be fine. She is also amazed and delighted about Comfort's impending motherhood.

"I know it's awful and disappointing about Snowstorm, but what would you have done if you had made it in time?" Ronnie asks gently. "You can't afford to buy another pony, anyway, least of all Snowstorm."

"I know. You're right, of course, but even so –"

"At least Comfort is going to be fine. I wonder who

the father of Comfort's foal is? Maybe it's a famous show jumper or a racehorse?"

"More likely some local farmer's stallion," I reply.

It is fun speculating about the foal, what he or she will be like, and I try not to think about the extra bills we will incur with a second pony. I only hope we can afford to keep two ponies that won't be able to earn their keep – for a long time to come.

When I go home, Mark is there, sitting next to Silke in the kitchen. As I am still feeling sorry for myself, I assume he has come to see Silke (who, incidentally, I have forgotten all about). But in fact he says that as soon as his father had told him what had happened he rushed over to see if I was all right. I am touched, if a little surprised. Maybe it's just an excuse. I'm in a suspicious frame of mind.

I tell him about Snowstorm, and how I will probably never see her again.

"Not that you would care," I add, bitterly.

Mark looks hurt and I know at once I shouldn't have said this.

"If that's how you feel, then I had better go," he replies angrily. Silke hurries after him, and I am left feeling more depressed than ever.

With Comfort out of action, it looks as if there will be no

riding all week. I go to the stable every day to help with Comfort, who seems to be doing well now, while Silke usually stays at home. I can't understand her reluctance to ride, and every time I tackle her about it, she changes the subject.

Spike has to go to France for a few days with her parents because their agent has found some houses he wants them to look at. She is really fed up with it. Then I get the stomach flu, so all in all it's not the best week. However, on Thursday night, Mark's dad asks if we would like to exercise some of the riding school ponies the following morning because they haven't been out much. Actually I think he feels sorry for us and is just being nice, but we all shriek, "Yes, please!" like pony-mad children (including Ronnie, who has somehow persuaded her Mom that she is well enough to come to the stables again). There are four ponies that need exercise, but with Spike out of action there are now only three of us. Then Gina has a brilliant idea.

"Why don't you bring Silke? You said she rode and she hasn't really had a chance yet."

"She doesn't seem that interested," I reply. "In fact, I wonder if she made up all that stuff about looking after a pony. Perhaps she can't ride at all."

"Well, there is one way to find out," insists Gina. "Ask her."

So at breakfast, I say to Silke, "We are all going for a trail ride today. Would you like to join us?"

If I am not mistaken, a look of panic – fear, even, crosses her face. She is not crazy about the idea.

"Well, I was going to take a trip into town, to a museum, perhaps –"

"We'd love to have you join us," I interrupt, adding, as a lever, "And actually, we would really appreciate it, because we are one rider short, with Spike away, so you would be doing Mark's dad a favor."

At Mark's name, she appears a little more interested. However, she is still hesitant and needs further persuasion.

"I had *so* hoped we would get to ride together," I continue, in a slightly whining voice. "I will be so disappointed if –"

"Oh, all right then," she replies, giving in somewhat ungraciously. "But I do not want to ride a frisky pony. Something quiet, please."

She disappears upstairs to get changed while I wash the breakfast things and returns ten minutes later in immaculate jodhpurs, which look as if they haven't been worn in ages, and a smart helmet and long polished boots. Suddenly I feel scruffy in my favorite lived-in black jodhpurs and faded sweatshirt. Still, at last I am going to see Silke ride. As you can imagine, I am very *curious*.

We collect Ronnie from next door and then meet Gina at the stables, where she has already tacked up Elliott and Polo.

"Great to see you, Silke," she smiles. "It's a good day for a ride. The sky is bright and clear, for once."

While Ronnie fetches Soames, I lead out Cy, the frisky bay, who decides to show off by giving a little buck when I tighten the girth. I notice that Silke goes a little pale.

"Don't worry," I reassure her. "You can ride Soames, who Ronnie is tacking up. He's as steady as an ox. He's ideal for beginners."

She gives me a funny look and I realize I have probably said the wrong thing. After all, from her letters Silke is hardly a beginner.

Gina leads Polo to the mounting block and gets on while I hold Cy, who is in a silly mood and tries to step on my foot, and Elliott. Ronnie then brings Soames over to the mounting block and hands the reins over to Silke.

"Don't worry, he's really quiet," she says, sensing Silke's unease.

She takes Elliott from me and mounts, and after dancing around the yard twice with one foot in the stirrup and the other doing a kind of hop, I scramble onto Cy in a rather undignified fashion.

Silke hasn't mounted yet so Gina offers to hold Soames while she gets on.

She sits well in the saddle, I notice, but fiddles unnecessarily with the stirrups, repeatedly adjusting them, until Gina finally says, "Well, are we ready?"

Gina leads the procession down the lane, Ronnie follows on Elliott, I go next with Cy and Silke and Soames stay at the back because Soames hates other ponies behind him and is liable to kick.

We stay in single file as we walk down the lane and then break into a trot to cross the road onto the track by the edge of the woods. I can see that Gina is heading for the common, where I imagine she is keen to try a few of the natural obstacles there because Polo has a terrific jump.

I am a little anxious about Silke, and when I glance back I see that she and Soames seem to be lagging behind.

"Kick on," I shout.

Silke closes her legs around Soames's not insubstantial belly and he picks up speed, but I notice that she is holding him in at the same time, which is why he is finding it hard to keep up with us.

"Let's have a canter!" yells Gina, who is clearly enjoying

herself on Polo and suddenly we are spread out three abreast like the Three Musketeers. Once the others have started to canter, Cy follows quickly, without any aids from me at all, so anxious is he not to be left behind. Elliott canters steadily with a nice smooth stride. I don't dare look back to check on Silke because all my energies go into holding Cy so he doesn't break into a gallop. Finally, when Polo slows down, so do the others and I feel able to turn quickly to see Soames fighting for his head while Silke hangs onto the reins for grim life. I can't understand why she is doing this. From her seat, aids and posture in the saddle it is obvious that Silke is an experienced rider, and Soames is such a gentleman to ride.

Once we are all together again Gina says, "Shall we jump? Polo is getting lathered up just looking at those lovely logs and that ditch. Do you jump, Silke?"

Silke's taut expression tells me she does not really want to jump, even though the logs are low. However, she nods and Gina gathers up her reins.

"Let's go over in procession," I suggest. "That way, the ponies will just follow each other and that will make it easier for all of us." Of course, I meant Silke, which I think the others picked up on.

"OK," and Gina only has to cluck with her tongue and Polo is off, leaping the first log with a foot to spare, closely followed by Ronnie and Elliott. I wait until they have taken the ditch before I ask Cy, who needs no persuading, to follow. He takes off much too soon but we land safely and he gathers himself up for the next one. For a moment I am so taken up with the exhilaration of flying through the air that I forget about Silke. When I do think about her, I tell myself that she is perfectly safe with Soames, who is used to teaching beginners to jump. Cy canters over the ditch and I join Gina and Ronnie to watch Silke.

She is still circling Soames before the first log and he shakes his head, confused.

"What is she doing?" wonders Gina aloud.

"Why didn't she say that she didn't want to jump?" adds Ronnie.

"She seems very nervous," I observe.

At that moment, Silke finally gives Soames more rein and he bounces towards the log. He stretches his neck ready to take off but, at the last minute, Silke suddenly jabs him in the mouth. Gamely, he tries to take off, but, realizing he can't make it, he skids to a halt and Silke, not surprisingly, goes flying over his head, landing on the ground with a sickening thud.

"Poor Soames," mutters Gina, shaking her head. We expect Silke to get up and brush herself off. But she doesn't move. Soames stands over her like a worried parent, staring down with a look of surprise.

It is rare for someone to fall off Soames. Small children are entrusted to him because of his gentle nature with people (although he isn't crazy about his fellow equines).

"Oh, God," I exclaim, visions of Silke being carted off to the hospital at the front of my mind. I imagine her parents phoning mine, telling my Mom how they had entrusted the care of their daughter to us and how we had repaid them by allowing her to be injured.

I leap off Cy and fling the reins to Gina. Ronnie rushes over to Silke with me.

"Silke, are you all right?" I burble in worried tones. She is lying awkwardly with her arm underneath her chest.

"I think so," she murmurs, rubbing her hand across her face and it looks as if she has been crying.

"Thank goodness she's OK," says Ronnie, and I also heave a sigh of relief.

We help her to her feet. "You're not hurt, are you? You're still in one piece," I tell her.

"Will you be able to get back on?" asks Gina, who has ridden over to join us, leading our mounts behind her.

A long silence follows, as if Silke is thinking very

carefully about this question. Then, to our surprise she starts to laugh.

"Yes. Yes, I think I *can* get back on," she replies. "Thank you."

I'm not sure why she's thanking us, exactly, but I am aware that something has changed, because when we ride back, Silke no longer holds Soames on a tight rein. She seems much more relaxed and, in fact, I can't help admiring her now confident riding style.

Silke seems more relaxed all around after this, although I still feel that there are things she isn't telling me. I'm pleased that she's ridden with us, though, and look forward to spending more time together for the remainder of the vacation. She offers to lend me one of her new lycra miniskirts for the party and is delighted when I accept.

"I will wear mine, too," she says with enthusiasm. "We can pretend to be sisters." She has an infectious giggle, and I laugh too.

After taking care of Comfort, we spend Saturday afternoon messing about with clothes and make-up and I realize Silke can be fun to be with. I team up the black lycra skirt (which is *very* short) with black tights and a simple white T-shirt. Silke does my make-up, which she is very good at, and I blow dry my hair, for once. I study myself in the mirror. I am really too short for the skirt, which makes my legs look a bit stumpy, but on the whole I look quite reasonable. Silke, on the other hand looks absolutely *stunning* in the miniskirt, which she wears with shimmery tights and a red halter neck top. Her hair is shining and her make-up is perfect. All in all, she's a knockout.

Just before we're about to leave, I take one last peek in the mirror, just in time to notice a big red pimple on my chin. It is too late do anything other than dab a bit of concealer on it, which has the effect of making it stand out like a shiny red beacon. I don't think Silke has ever has a pimple in her entire life.

As soon as we arrive, Mark rushes over to greet us.

"You look great," he says, addressing the remark to both of us, but looking at Silke. "Hey, Matty, you don't usually wear a miniskirt," he remarks. "Is it new?"

"Silke lent it to me," I reply, suddenly feeling self-conscious.

Then he promptly whisks Silke off to introduce her to his friends from the jazz club. I did meet them once before, ages ago, at a concert, so I assume this is why Mark feels it's OK to abandon me. I wish that Ronnie were here to talk to, but after our ride yesterday her throat felt bad again, and her mom has made her stay in bed, even though she wanted to come to the party.

"Enjoying yourself, Matty?" Gina looks pretty, as usual, with her neat hair and simple black dress.

I shrug. "Only just got here. Too early to say."

"Well you could sound a bit more enthusiastic. Mark has gone to a lot of trouble. There are some tasty little nibble things in the kitchen and delicious cake. I really like his house. It's a pity Spike isn't coming."

"Poor Spike."

"Yes. Poor Spike."

We stand together, studying the other guests, some of whom we recognize from the stables, others who are new faces to us.

"You look nice, Matty. That skirt suits you."

"What, with my legs?" I reply ungraciously. "And don't say you haven't noticed the fresh zit on my chin. Great timing."

Gina looks annoyed. "Don't be crazy, Matty. No one will notice. Anyway, if you're going to be a grouch all night, I'll go and talk to someone else."

"Sorry, Gina."

Then I notice that Silke and Mark are dancing together. The music is very rhythmic and I have to admit that she's a very good dancer. Much better than I am. I realize that I'm feeling jealous.

Matters are not helped when Gina whispers, "Don't you think that Silke is flirting with Mark? If he were my boyfriend, I wouldn't like it one bit."

I find myself studying every move that Silke makes, every smile and look that they exchange. I can feel my face getting redder by the minute.

So when they go outside together, I find myself following them. I watch from a distance and at first they just seem to be talking intently. Then they sit down next to each other on the garden bench, and Mark puts his arm around Silke and...

I can stand it no longer.

"How could you?" I explode, confronting them. "I thought you were supposed to be my friends. I should have known you were cheating on me. I hate you both!"

I continue shouting and hurling insults. Then, after I have burst into tears, I return to the house, grab my coat and storm out. I run all the way home.

I wish that Silke had never come to stay. Mark and I were getting along great until she arrived. Not only that, but soon Spike will leave, and I'll probably never see Snowstorm ever again. I am consumed with self-pity. And to top it all off, I have an ugly red zit erupting like Vesuvius on my chin!

Chapter 8

Luckily, when I get back home, Mom and Dad are watching television, so I am able to sneak in without having to run the gauntlet of Mom's questioning. (She will mean well, but I can't face it at the moment.) I am tempted to throw Silke's things out of the window, and I certainly feel entitled to have my own bed back tonight. I practically tear off the clothes that Silke lent me and replace them with my grungiest jeans and sweater.

Peering at myself in the mirror I notice that my eyes are red and puffy and streaked black with mascara from where I have been crying. The spot on my chin is still there, mocking me. I am hardly aware of the knock on the door until Mom shouts up the stairs, "Matty, I think you should come down. Right now!"

To my surprise, Silke and Mark are sitting in the kitchen.

"Go away," I reply (although the actual words I use are somewhat stronger). Mom looks shocked but tactfully leaves us alone.

"We need to explain," begins Mark.

"There's nothing to explain, you rotten two-timer." I practically spit the words out.

"You've got the wrong idea, Matty," says Silke.

"Yeah, right," I reply.

Suddenly Mark sounds annoyed. He grabs my arm. "Look, why don't you just sit down and listen for once. Hear us out."

I glare at him and push him away. I won't sit down, but I lean against the sink and fold my arms. "OK. Go ahead. Tell me why I've gotten it all wrong."

"Mark is not two-timing you, Matty," insists Silke. "We just get along well. That is all."

"You think that I'm going to buy that? I don't believe you. I saw you cuddled up together. You certainly *were* getting along well."

"Silke was upset. I was comforting her. I wasn't doing anything wrong." Mark sounds adamant, and I'm getting really angry now.

"You must think I'm an idiot," I retort.

"When you behave like this, I *do* think that," says Mark. "Look, Silke was upset because she had a big fight with her brother before she left Germany. They are

102

very close and it was preying on her mind. She hated leaving home without sorting things out with him. I was consoling her."

I grunt in response.

"I let Silke phone him at his art school from the house after you left the party. They have made things up, now."

"I'm so glad," I reply sarcastically.

Silke looks embarrassed.

"You don't need to be so aggressive, Matty," adds Mark. "In fact, if you must know, Silke has been feeling miserable most of the time she's been staying with you. She thinks you don't like her even though she's tried hard to fit in, and now she's so unhappy she wants to go home."

Mark is standing protectively by Silke's side.

I am staggered. "But that's crazy," I respond defensively. I am *not* letting them turn this around so it looks like it's all my fault.

"It isn't surprising that Silke feels that," adds Mark. "After all, you haven't spent much time with her since she arrived. You must admit that."

"Yes, but I've had a lot on my mind, and Silke doesn't seem to be interested in what I do, and..." My voice trails off as I try to take in what is being said. "Is this true, Silke? Are you really so fed up?"

Then suddenly we all start to talk truthfully and say what we feel.

I tell Silke that I expected her to want to ride and spend all her time at the stables with me, and she says that she didn't think I wanted her company, particularly when I sent her off to town with Mark.

"It made me feel as if you didn't want me around," she informs me.

"Well, I didn't," I confess, "But only because I didn't want to drag you around doing something you didn't want to do. Besides," I add, "You seemed pretty keen to go out with Mark instead."

"I didn't want to offend anyone or appear rude," she replies. "And I did have a nice time with Mark."

"Yes, I could see that. I was jealous."

"Jealous of me?" she responds, genuinely surprised. "I think it is the other way around. I'm a bit jealous of you."

Now it's my turn to be surprised. "Why should you be jealous of me?"

"You have such a nice family, and lots of people around you and real friends, and," she pauses and smiles sheepishly, "a gorgeous boyfriend."

We both turn to look at Mark, who is blushing furiously. "I think I'll leave you two girls to chat," he says abruptly disappearing into the yard, and Silke and I dissolve into giggles.

We're both feeling better by now, so I put the kettle on and Silke catches my arm, saying, "I am sorry if you thought I was going after Mark. He is a very attractive person, and I must admit that I did flirt with him. I enjoyed having so much attention for a change."

I recall our conversation on the way to the stables when Silke explained that she was used to her own company with her parents being away a lot. She hadn't talked about her friends, not even the one whose pony she was looking after. She had sounded lonely and I began to understand why she had behaved the way she did.

"But you must know, Matty, that although Mark was very flattered by my interest, you are the one that he cares for."

She sounds so sincere that I want to believe her. But still, at the back of mind it is hard to overcome my doubts. What boy in his right mind wouldn't prefer Silke to me?

"Also," she continues, "I have you to thank for being able to ride again."

"What do you mean?" I am puzzled by this.

"A few weeks ago I had a bad fall on my friend's pony," she explains. "It was very frightening. Starchaser is usually so well-behaved, but we had to cross a busy road and a truck went past with a heavy load which was not secured properly. Starchaser panicked when part of the load fell off and crashed onto the road. He just bolted, right in front of the oncoming traffic. How we managed not to get hit, I don't know. But when I finally stopped him, half a mile up the road, I was shaking so much I just couldn't get back on. My nerve had gone. I walked him home and, although I tried to ride him the next day, he sensed my worry and started to misbehave. My friend, who doesn't have time to ride him now because she is working long hours, was understanding at first but soon got impatient with me because he wasn't getting any exercise. So, just before I left Germany, she told me she has loaned Starchaser out to someone else. It has spoiled our friendship and I haven't ridden since."

"Oh, Silke, that must have been awful," I respond sympathetically. She had really had a rough time of it lately – and it appeared that I had added to it! I had heard before of very experienced riders losing their nerve, and tried to imagine how frustrating it must be. Of course, now I could understand why she had been so reluctant to ride – and why at the same time her letters had stopped mentioning ponies. She must have been upset at losing Starchaser.

"But why didn't you tell me?" I ask.

"How could I?" she replies sheepishly. "I knew you were pony mad and I had so looked forward to coming here. I thought you wouldn't want me to come if you thought I couldn't ride. It wasn't that I didn't *want* to ride. I *did* want to ride. I was just scared. So I thought I could just bluff. But I still brought my riding gear, in case the worse came to the worse."

"Oh, Silke, you silly thing. I would have wanted to help." I tried to sound jokey, but inside I was stricken with guilt for the way I had behaved towards her.

"But you *did* help me, by making me ride with you yesterday. I'm not sure I could have tackled riding again without your cajoling. I was angry that you tried to bully me into it, but I am so glad that you did. Part of my reluctance was the fear of falling off again, which is exactly what happened. But when it did happen, it made me realize that it wasn't nearly as bad as I imagined."

"So now we can ride together again?" I venture.

"Of course," she replies, smiling.

We join Mark in the back yard to drink our cocoa, and I'm glad that we've cleared the air. Perhaps we can all make a fresh start. But there is yet another revelation.

"We know how upset you've been about Snowstorm and what a difficult time it's been for you recently," says Mark. "So we've been thinking about how we can help."

"Here," says Silke, triumphantly waving a piece of paper at me. On it is an address. "The man who bought Snowstorm."

I want to leap into the air and yell for joy.

"Oh, Mark. But how...?"

"It was Silke's idea. She overheard your phone conversation and found the phone number of the woman who was selling Snowstorm on the telephone stand, where you left it. She knew that you weren't able to find out where Snowstorm went, so we had a little chat and she suggested that I call up and pretend that I was a policeman and say that Snowstorm had been reported stolen! It really knocked the wind out of that woman, and she quickly told me the name and address of the man who had bought her."

I began to feel very foolish. They *did* care about what I had been going through after all.

"Now that you have the address, what will you do when you find Snowstorm?" asks Silke.

I shrug. "I don't know. Except that I want to make sure that she's all right."

"I can understand how you feel," says Silke. "I know what it is like to lose a pony."

Mark is looking very serious and I think he realizes, perhaps for the first time, just how important Snowstorm is to me.

"Thank you both for this," I say gratefully, clutching the piece of paper. "I'll go today."

"Then we'll come with you. If you think it'll help," says Mark.

The address is on the other side of the next town, not far from an industrial park, so we all travel on the bus. As we approach the address, Mark recognizes it as a dealer's yard.

"I think Dad brought me here once, when we were looking for a second pony. It's a respectable yard, so you shouldn't worry about Snowstorm," he reassures me, adding, "If she's still here. Dealers often have a high turnover. They like to shift stock as soon as they buy it, to maximize their profit. They won't want to spend money on keeping a pony if they can resell quickly." It all sounds so clinical, like buying and selling tins of beans rather than living creatures. I can't bear to think that someone would regard Snowstorm as some kind of "product." Mark senses my unease and adds quickly, "I'm sure Snowstorm will still be here; after all, it's only been a week since she was sold."

I know he's only trying to make me feel better, but he doesn't sound convinced. The words *only a week* resound in my ears. It feels like a lifetime to me. I think it has been one of the worst weeks of my life. (Little was I prepared for what was to come.)

There are several fields backing onto one another, separated by an electric fence, filled with horses and ponies of all shapes and sizes. It's a sunny day and they're standing in groups, head to tail, swishing the flies away. I strain my eyes to see if Snowstorm is among them, but I'm unable to spot her. My heart sinks. Maybe Mark is right; maybe we're too late.

"He probably got Snowstorm for a good price if her owners needed to make a quick sale," Mark observes.

A gaunt looking man wearing a tweed jacket and cap comes over to greet us, a yapping terrier at his feet.

"Afternoon. And how can I help you?" His speech is ponderous and he sounds very tired.

We look awkwardly at one another and I realize we should have prepared what we were going to say. We are supposed to be serious buyers looking for a pony.

"We are after a gray," I begin.

"I have several grays," the dealer replies, indicating that we follow him.

"Any particular type?"

"Welsh, with a good jump," Mark continues, following my lead.

"I have just the thing," says the dealer, leading us into a large, airy barn with rows of stalls separated by rope. My stomach fills with butterflies.

"This is a nice little mare," says the dealer, indicating a well-built dapple gray. My heart sinks. It's not Snowstorm.

He notes our disappointment. "You after something different, then? She's a very handy pony, well-mannered."

"Not for me," I say shaking my head. This feels unreal. I'm behaving as if I have come to buy a pony. It is quite bizarre.

"Let me see now, I have a gray gelding over in the top field."

"It has to be a mare," I insist.

"Well, I only have one other gray mare, but she belongs to my son and isn't for sale."

"Could we see her anyway?" I insist.

He shrugs. "OK. But like I say, she isn't for sale."

He leads us over to a small stable block behind the barn.

"Well, this is Melody," he says, shooting the bolts back on the bottom half of the door so I can go inside. "My boy took an instant shine to her, he did, the moment she arrived. Expects to win a few prizes. She's a great jumper."

The gray mare is standing in the far corner of the stall, her head hanging low, picking at a dry bundle of hay. She doesn't look at us, doesn't respond at all.

"Come on, girl," says the dealer encouragingly, clicking his tongue. But he has to go inside and take her head collar before she'll look up. Her eyes are dull, but when I see her face I recognize her at once.

I look across at Mark and my eyes fill with tears. Looking at Snowstorm now makes it hard to remember the super fit pony in the peak of condition that Mark sold last year.

She seems tired, and I notice with alarm that she has two recent cuts across her knees.

The dealer follows my gaze. "Accident in the horse trailer. Pony got scared."

He leads her outside and she is very sluggish. I can see that Mark is shocked.

"If you aren't so insistent on a gray I have plenty of other nice ponies that you could consider," says the dealer, trying to persuade us.

I can't bear it. This was not what I had expected. I had thought I would be seeing Snowstorm, been reassured that she was well, and then gone through the agony of walking away again. But I know that now I can't walk away.

"I want to buy this pony," I stammer.

"I told you," the dealer replies sharply. "She belongs to my son. He thinks the world of her."

I want to argue with him, but Mark gives me a warning glare.

"Look, since the pony belongs to my son perhaps you should be having this conversation with him," suggests the dealer. "He's in the barn. I'll give him a call. Danny! Come over here!"

A stocky boy who looks about sixteen appears from the barn and strolls across to us, hands in his pocket, clearly not in a hurry.

"Danny, this young woman is interested in buying Melody," his father explains.

The boy laughs. "Sell Melody? No way. She's going to win me the County Jumping Championship."

"See? I told you," mutters the dealer, shaking his head. "Well, if I can't interest you in another pony..."

"Thank you for your time," says Mark, sounding resigned.

"But Mark –" I protest as he grabs my arm and practically drags me away, with Silke at my side. I can tell from the look on her face that she shares my distress.

As we walk away I hear the boy mumble something to his father before disappearing into the stable with Melody. Unfortunately, we have quite a long wait for the bus. The bus stop is halfway down the lane, with a clear view of the field. And as if to rub salt into the wound, while we're waiting, we can see the boy bring Snowstorm out into the field for some jumping practice.

He's not a skilled rider like Mark and favors the push and pull style of riding. He also carries a crop, which makes me cringe. We all watch, horrified, as he tries to make Snowstorm jump, digging his heels into her once sensitive sides and hauling on her soft mouth. Instead of leaving it to Snowstorm to judge the best place to take off, which is what works best with her, he interferes, throwing her off stride so she pecks at the last minute. Somehow, though, she manages to scramble over the jumps, with additional encouragement from the crop. I can't bear it.

Just when I am ready to explode, the bus arrives.

"We have to go now," says Mark reluctantly but I can see he doesn't want to.

"We can't go," I say, trembling. "Not without Snowstorm."

The bus is starting to brake and the doors open.

"So what do you suggest?" snaps Mark, visibly upset.

"I don't know. We just can't leave."

The bus driver waits for us to board, drumming his fingers impatiently.

"We have to buy her back. We have to make them sell," I say desperately.

"We've tried," sighs Mark.

"Not hard enough."

"Are you youngsters planning to get on this bus today or not?" remarks the bus driver sharply. "I do have other customers waiting further down the road, you know."

Mark steps forward, but he is hesitating. The next bus won't be for another hour.

"Well?" repeats the bus driver. "What is it to be? Are you getting on, or are you staying here?"

Chapter 9

As the bus disappears down the road, I know we've made the right decision. We can't just leave Snowstorm.

"If they won't sell, we'll steal her," I insist.

"Oh, that sounds like a sensible idea," retorts Mark sarcastically. "Well done, Matty."

I ignore him and continue, "Anyway it won't be stealing – it'll be rescuing."

"Honestly, Matty, sometimes –"

Luckily, Silke intervenes. "Look, perhaps we should try again. Maybe we *can* persuade the boy to sell Snowstorm to us. We mustn't give up."

"Thank you Silke," I say gratefully.

Mark shrugs. "I suppose it's worth one more try."

We walk briskly back to the yard. I can see that the dealer is hoping there won't be any trouble.

This time he seems to weaken. "Well, it's obvious

you are very interested, so I'll have another word with the boy."

He strides across the field and shouts to his son. The boy yanks at Snowstorm's head and trots her roughly back to the gate. They talk for a while, poor Snowstorm standing with head hanging. Eventually they come over.

"We might be able to come to an agreement, after all," begins the boy, and I am wary of the tone in his voice.

"Good," says Mark hopefully. Then comes the crunch. "How much are you asking?"

"Well..." The boy pauses, as if deep in thought before naming an exorbitant price.

"That's outrageous," replies Mark, aghast.

"I thought you wanted to buy her." The boy sounds irritated.

I am overwhelmed with despair. Of course, it doesn't matter whether or not he wants a hundred dollars or a thousand, because I haven't got a spare bean. I look across at Mark, my eyes pleading.

"I can't afford that," he says.

Danny shrugs. "Well, you've got a problem, then, don't you?"

"Perhaps we can negotiate," offers Mark, but Danny is adamant.

"That's the price I want. Take it or leave it."

By now, my heart has sunk into my boots and I am in the depths of despair. I look at poor Snowstorm and want so much to touch her and reassure her. Then, to my amazement, Mark says, "OK. It's a deal."

I stare at him, open-mouthed. I can't believe I'm hearing this.

"But I can't give you the money now," he adds. "I'll have to come back later tomorrow."

Danny grunts suspiciously. "Well, if you want to secure the deal you had better leave a deposit on her."

"Agreed," says Mark and we frantically discuss what we could leave as a deposit. Between the three of us, just the change for the bus fare home!

"Here, take this," says Silke suddenly, and she pulls a gold signet ring from her finger. "This is worth at least a quarter of the price you want."

"Silke!" I am overwhelmed by her generosity.

"Don't worry, Matty," she smiles. "I will get it back tomorrow when we collect Snowstorm."

Leaving Snowstorm behind is the hardest thing in the world, but at least there is hope in my heart, although where Mark is planning to get the money is beyond me.

We are in a more positive frame of mind when we make the return journey to the stables.

"Are you planning to borrow the money from your dad?" I ask Mark.

He shakes his head. "He's put everything we've got into the Old Fort Riding School. He needs all his money to pay back a bank loan."

"Even if I scraped together all of my savings there wouldn't be nearly enough to buy Snowstorm," I mutter. "And my parents haven't any spare cash."

Suddenly Mark takes my hand and squeezes it tightly. He smiles. "Don't worry, Matty. I know how I'll raise the money."

It's hard to get through the rest of the day. Even so, there is work to be done with Comfort, and this time Silke is on hand to help me. Mark disappears but promises that he will meet us back at the stables the next afternoon, when he has arranged to collect Snowstorm. His dad has agreed to bring the horse trailer.

When Silke, Mark and I make the journey back to the dealer's yard, I am terrified that something will go wrong. What if Danny sells her to someone else? What if he changes his mind altogether and decides not to sell her at all? These thoughts infiltrate my mind and I think Mark can guess that I'm concerned.

"Don't worry," he reassures. "Everything will be fine."

It occurs to me that he is probably as upset about Snowstorm as I am; after all, she was his pony and he probably feels bad about where she has ended up.

Then we pull into the yard and the dealer appears. There is no sign of Danny.

"He's out with his pals," explains the dealer. "Left me to conclude the arrangements."

I'm relieved that Danny isn't around when Mark counts out the cash.

The dealer writes out a receipt, gives Silke back her ring and then goes to fetch Snowstorm.

I wonder if we should expect problems loading her, bearing in mind what the dealer had said earlier about how she sustained the injuries to her knees. But she just seems very subdued and plods up the ramp without any trouble. Mark's dad closes the door and we are ready to leave.

"She's yours now, Matty," says Mark.

The words *she's yours now* echo in my ears like the most beautiful sound on earth. I can hardly believe it. I have always wanted her and now, finally, it has happened.

"But Mark, you bought her, and –"

"She belongs to you," Mark says firmly. "You can pay me back, in installments," he jokes.

"Thank you, Mark."

119

At last it has happened. Snowstorm is mine. My dream has come true.

We are taking Snowstorm back to the Old Fort. We are bringing her home at last. I am in a daze the whole journey back.

Gina has prepared a stable for Snowstorm, banked high with fresh straw. I lead her out in triumph and she pricks her ears for the first time and seems quite alert.

"She is taking more of an interest in her surroundings," remarks Silke.

"It might be a while before she begins to eat properly and her coat improves," warns Mark. "But good feeding and proper care will bring her back to the way she used to be."

I know that he is right.

It's a long time before I leave Snowstorm that evening. When I've finished hugging and kissing her, I stay with her in the stable, just talking, telling her of all the things that have happened since she went away. Before I go, she looks into my eyes and I think that at last I see a glimmer of recognition there.

"You're home now," I tell her. "And I will give you all the love and attention you deserve."

It's dark by now, and the half moon sends a pretty silvery

glow over the surrounding fields. It is quite magical, really, watching the ponies in the moonlight, and I'm briefly reminded of Socrates, our Moonlight Horse, and the night I was alone with him when the Fort was derelict; the night I was convinced I saw a ghost. It seems like such a long time ago, like a dream.

I decide to look in on Comfort, who is round and contented, nibbling sweet fresh hay in a comfortable stable. I wonder again what her foal will be like. It's funny how things turn out. I had always wanted a pony, and now I have two – with another on the way! I am so happy that I refuse to think about how we will afford to look after them all!

The rest of the vacation seems to go by in a flash; days filled with riding out with Silke and my friends, caring for Comfort, and getting Snowstorm fit again. The first time that I ride her again is a strange experience, and I wonder if I will feel disappointed. But she has not forgotten anything, and as soon as I give her the proper aids, she eagerly obliges and is so wonderful I wish I could stay in the saddle forever.

Mark and I come to a financial arrangement over Snowstorm. He only wants me to pay back half the money he paid for her and wants to share the costs of her care and upkeep with me, although he still has no desire to ride again. She is soon such a popular working boarder that she earns not only her keep but that of Comfort as well! Admittedly, it is very hard for me to allow other people to ride her, but Mark's dad promises faithfully that only the experienced riders can use her and, after a while, I stop supervising them and begin to trust other people with her.

Spike comes back from France jubilant, to our amazement.

"We're not moving after all," she exclaims, so pleased she can hardly get the words out. "Dad has decided to turn down the new job!"

"What happened?" we ask, curious to know what could have changed.

"Well, while we were looking at houses there he struck up a conversation with the agent, who happened to mention that the company Dad would be working for has been involved in unethical activities in the region, with shady land deals. Dad made further inquiries and as a result declared he wanted nothing more to do with the company. So, we're staying here, Dad still has his old job, and they've promoted him, because they're worried about losing him again. Everything is back to normal."

"That's wonderful," says Gina, and we all agree.

"It's good to have you back, Spike."

It is the day before Silke's return home and we are all sitting in the tack room chatting – Silke, Mark, Gina, Spike, Ronnie and I.

"I think we should have another party," says Mark. "To celebrate Snowstorm's return, and Spike's good news. We'll have it tomorrow – before Silke has to go."

"I think that's a great idea, Mark," says Spike and everyone agrees.

And this time, it really is a great party. With no more misunderstandings I can enjoy myself with Mark and Silke without feeling jealous (well, only a little. She is prettier than I am, after all!)

Silke and I part the best of friends, and I actually miss her when she's gone. So when I get a postcard from her, inviting me to stay with her for a few weeks in the summer, I'm delighted.

"She's decided to get another pony on loan," I tell Mark, reading the postcard out loud to him. We are lying on the grass in my back yard and the sun is shining.

"I'm glad," he replies. "Silke was really good with horses. Natural affinity."

"You did like Silke a lot, didn't you?" I say casually.

"Yes, she was a very attractive girl."

"More attractive than I am?" I ask playfully.

"Oh, yes, *much* more attractive than boring old you," he replies, his tone serious. "And I was flattered by her attentions."

For a moment I begin to wonder... and then he grins, grabs me and, to my surprise, plants a great big kiss on my chin.

"You're the only one for me, Matty," he laughs. "Even if you *do* get zits!"

"Mark," I begin cautiously. "I have a question that's been eating into me for ages. How did you raise the money to buy Snowstorm?"

"I robbed a bank," he laughs. "Seriously, do you really want to know?"

I nod.

"OK, then, I'll tell you. I sold my new clarinet."

"Oh, Mark." I am dumbstruck. "I know how much that clarinet meant to you."

He shrugs. "And I know how much Snowstorm means to you."

So Silke was right after all. It really is true love.